A Disgusting Supermarket of DEATH

James C. Harberson III

FIRST PRINTING, February 2021.
Harry Markos, Director.

Paperback: ISBN 978-1-913802-24-0
eBook: ISBN 978-1-913802-25-7

Book design by: Ian Sharman

Cover art and design by: Stephen Baskerville

www.markosia.com

First Edition

∾CONTENTS∾

11. **Swatted**: SWAT officers start murdering their colleagues and each other shortly after killing a family during a botched raid.

12. **A Good Scare**: An extreme haunted house patron can't tell if the murders occurring around him are real or just part of the entertainment.

13. **Spring Chickens**: A kid searching for his missing friend discovers that residents of the neighboring retirement home are sacrificing orphans to bathe in their blood.

14. **Medical Malpractice**: A group of healthcare providers arrange a massive car pile-up so they can murder the victims.

15. **Ghosts of Who I Never Was**: A clone scheduled for termination escapes her captors, not knowing that she harbors a serial killer's identity and homicidal urges.

16. **Due Process**: Murder results when three school friends try to rein in a misbehaving classmate by putting him on trial.

17. **Dream Job**: Producers of a show in which convicted serial killers comment on schlocky horror films receive a mysterious, untitled film that appears disturbingly real.

18. **Chemotherapy**: An overeager life coach virtually stalks and abuses her clients to "improve" them.

19. **Number Six**: While investigating several ghastly murders, a homicide detective kills people he's supposed to help.

20. **Unforbidden Knowledge**: A reporter attends an invitation-only screening of a horror film that drives viewers to murder and/or suicide.

21. **Team Player**: A freshman invited to join America's winningest high school football team discovers he must enter a blood pact with Satan to do so.

22. **Peak Bliss**: A man living in endless luxury provided by doting robots finds himself dead to joy and therefore suicidal.

Special Thanks:
Margaret Harberson
James C. Harberson, Jr.
Justin Harberson
Harry Markos
Stephen Baskerville
Aviva Abramovsky
Debbie Bookstaber
Thomas Crowell
Matt Gold
Irina Manta
Will Meyerhofer
Frazer Rice
David Rothschild

EXTRA CREDIT

"Do you really know him? Hodgepodge?"

"Yes. I deal with him quite often."

"What's he like?"

It was another true crime convention, this one in Omaha. And it was January. My stomach objected to the motel coffee and plastic-coated pastry. The middle-aged shut in crowding me smelled like the last five pizza burritos he'd microwaved. He wore a hoodie featuring an infamous mug shot of Kleber "Hodgepodge" Pillsbury, a gadabout mass-murderer who penned a series of bestselling memoirs weaving lurid recollections of his crimes with pro-eugenics jeremiads and detailed ratings of past lovers. (To his dismay, all profits went to his victims' families, thanks to an activist court that pissed on the First Amendment.) Kleber got the nickname "Hodgepodge" after he merged several victims into one body and delivered the results to a prominent medical school, which kept it alive for almost two weeks.

"He's a serial killer. We keep and feed him at the minimum the Constitution permits. It's like having a pet scorpion you don't want but can't get rid of."

"I know! What's he like?"

"He's a hopeless narcissist utterly incapable of empathy; however, he has a felicitous prose style that wins him admirers notwithstanding those failings."

Crime cons are a series of weirdness filters. Just paying to go was weird or borderline weird (the idly curious). Paying twenty-five hundred to hear me was plenty weird. Staying to ask questions, weirder still. The four stragglers before me were maximum weird: fleeting romantic relationships (if any); irregular employment; and extravagant devotion to murderers they lacked the fortitude and charisma to be. They all wore Hodgepodge T-shirts or other gear. Murray, the fatty in my face, had SK mugshot sleeve tattoos: Gein, Gacy, Manson, Fish, Kuklinski, Ramirez, and even the Columbine shooters.

The questions were inane and profound, guided by crushing teenager logic: "Does he wear cologne?"; "What's his favourite movie?"; "How big is his, well, you know—"

And then: "Can I meet him?"

The others asked the same.

I smiled. I mean, that's why I was there. Still, I had to go a little coquette. "That would be highly irregular."

"You're not saying 'No.'"

"There are security concerns."

"We'll sign any waiver you want."

"And no photos allowed. I mean, like I said, it's highly irregular. My superiors would object."

"Then you shouldn't tell them."

"Well, I wasn't planning on it. However, I'll have to involve some trusted personnel."

God they were eager: Ten thousand. Each.

They squirmed, but they agreed. Maybe I'd lowballed it. Maybe they got more of their parents' Social Security benefits than I'd guessed. Oh, well.

I collected their contact information and promised to call.

***

A police academy friend now working in Indiana ran them for me. They were pristinely crime-free, nobodies: Murray, 43, who spent his time acquiring online college degrees and maintaining *thickerthanwater.com*, a serial killer/mass murderer fan site; Georgina, 31, who sold homemade jewellery online when not cosplaying Lizzie Borden; Melanie, 37, a corporate secretary-cum-Aileen-Wuornos cosplaying dominatrix; and Jack, 26, a dweeby accountant who, according to his financials, was Melanie's best client.

None were married.

***

I had Officer Smith pick them up in my SUV. He was a guard and the facility's weed connection. He cut me into the profits and did me occasional favours, like picking up illegal meet and greeters for Hodgepodge. They really wanted to ride in an official prison van, but I didn't want to have to explain the mileage.

We met in an abandoned wing of the prison scheduled for demolition. No cameras, no barbed wire. Smith frisked them at the door, confiscating all electronic devices. I watched as he did.

"This shit isn't ending up on the tubes. It's totally private. And if you blab, Smith here will pay you a corrective visit."

Smith smiled. "True crime."

We assembled in the infirmary. Hodgepodge sat in an old wheelchair, handcuffs secured to a restraint belt chained to leg restraints chained to the floor. Just forty, he was sleek and handsome, his hair buzzed, his muscles bulging against his jumpsuit. "Hodge" was tattooed on the left forearm, "Podge" on the right.

Four folding chairs stood before him. I was in one corner, Smith in the other. We ate sliders from the catering station Smith had set up beforehand. They'd insisted on refreshments; I suppose their stomachs were hardened to just about anything.

Hodgepodge smiled at me. "Aren't you going to introduce us?"

I finished the slider, straightened my tie, and joined them.

"Um, okay. People, this is Kleber Pillsbury, popularly known as—"

They cheered: "Hodgepodge!"

Hodgepodge smiled.

"Well, you know who I am. Who are you—"

I interjected. "Sorry. First names only. And no signings, either. He disembowelled a guy with fountain pen right before they caught him."

Hodgepodge smiled.

Georgina panicked. "Can I at least read him the poem I wrote?"

"Uhh-"

Hodgepodge beamed. "Is it erotic?"

She blushed. "Well—"

"Then you MUST!" She extracted a crumpled paper from her pocket.

Jack frowned. "Wait, why does she get to go first?"

Hodgepodge turned to him. "One of the things one learns in prison is patience. You'll have an opportunity to question me, or confess to me, or indulge whatever other cryptic depravity powers your dreams—"

I smiled. "No touching—"

"Oh, Warden, pooping on my party as always, and not in the good way."

"His point is that you'll all have a chance to speak your peace, or whatever."

Melanie and Jack turned to me hopefully. "We wanted a private audience. We also wrote something, a kind of interpretive dance incorporating BDSM elements symbolizing the state's unwarranted oppression of Hodgepodge for affronting society's petit bourgeois—"

"No. And besides, Hodgepodge's restraints ensure that he can't indulge himself during this visitation."

Murray smirked. Hodgepodge smiled at him. "What's your name, All-Star?"

Murray looked at me. I nodded.

"Murray."

"Murray, you're a mousey one. I'm sure you paid as much as the others. Don't you have any special demands?"

He shook his head.

"I love your tunic."

Murray wore the Hodgepodge hoodie he'd worn to the Omaha crime con. He blushed.

"I'm perfectly restrained. Don't you want to smell me or lick me or something?"

He shook his head with embarrassment suggesting he did.

"Well, let me ask a question before we start."

They all straightened, eager pupils.

"How many of you have taken the Hare test?"

They blanched.

"C'mon, put up your hands!"

Melanie and Jack raised first. Then Georgina. Then Murray.

Smith looked at me. "What's that?"

Hodgepodge obliged. "The Hare Psychopathy Checklist-Revised is the gold standard maniac detector. Twenty questions scored on a three-point scale, zero to two, forty points max. It measures a combination of antisocial behaviours and personality traits. A score of thirty or above means the taker, is, well, disinclined to stay the stabby hand."

This was turning out to be more fun than I expected. "So—"

He smiled at Melanie and Jack. "Melanie! And Jack!"

"So, Melanie and Jack, are you summa, magna, or merely cum laude?"

Melanie smiled. "We're both thirty-threes."

Georgina interjected. "I'm thirty-four!"

"Bravo."

"How about you Murray?"

He said nothing.

"C'mon, All-Star. Give us your number."

Murray teared up; mascara stained his cheeks.

"Seventeen."

Hodgepodge frowned.

"I'm—I'm so sorry. I took it four times. Different shrinks each time. It was always the same."

"That's okay, Murray. That's okay. You're still beautiful on the outside."

"Really?"

"At least when you're wearing me."

Hodgepodge looked at the others. "Let's open this up to the group. What do you all think?"

Melanie sneered. "I think he's a fucking poser." The others nodded.

"I'm not! Really! Look!" He rose and removed his sweatshirt and the T-shirt underneath. Tattooed prominently across his chest was Hodgepodge's mugshot.

Hodgepodge smiled at the others. "C'mon, people, that kind of commitment is worth at least a few extra points, isn't it?"

They glowered at Murray.

Jack sneered. "This feels like affirmative action. I mean, let's be honest. He just hasn't got it, and we shouldn't pretend that he has just to make him feel better."

Hodgepodge smiled. "Well, test scores aren't everything. I mean, even I only got a thirty-eight. Perfect, that's none of us. How about you, Warden, what's your score?"

I flipped him off. He chuckled. "Besides, tests are for commies and Canadians. Who cares if you're a forty on paper if you're a zero on the field? I was raised in the Church of Jesus Christ of Latter-day Saints. Our favourite symbol isn't the cross. Americans don't do personal defeat. And, say what you like about Jesus, getting crucified was definitely a personal defeat. No, Mormons prefer the beehive, even though, as a patriarchy, the queen model of governance proves somewhat incongruous. But, whatever. The busy beehive, the unified purpose, conquering through cooperation, God Bless America, right?"

I rolled my eyes. Hodgepodge pursed his lips towards me. Then he smiled at Murray. "Fuck psychology. It's just bullshit flaunting fancy adjectives. Whatever you want, you just gotta hustle."

Hodgepodge removed his right shoe, little more than a slipper, with his left. He then slid it to Murray's feet. "So, Murray, it's time to, well, step up and fill these shoes. Er, shoe."

Murray retrieved the shoe and from it a straight razor. He trembled. "I—I don't know..."

"That's the seventeen talking, the little wannabe who's probably still a virgin except for that time he frottaged a plus-sized Elizabeth Bathory cosplayer when she was three Bloody Marys in. It's time for that guy to fuck off. If you kill Jack and Melanie and Georgina, nobody will ever care what your score was. They'll just know you as that guy that postaled some crime con losers too meek to own their depravity."

Georgina snarled. "We're not losers! We're enthusiasts!"

Murray snapped. He brandished the razor and, before she could protest, slashed Georgina's throat. She bucked, then gurgled, her blood spraying the others who were trying to process what was happening. Then he slipped in her blood while attacking Jack and Melanie, landing in Jack's lap.

"Sorry."

He gutted Jack, who slid from his chair onto the ground. Melanie screamed and kept screaming. And Murray, in a spot of comic relief, couldn't dislodge the razor, now stuck in Jack's sternum.

Hodgepodge laughed.

Murray surrendered the knife and charged Melanie.

Hodgepodge cheered. "Go, All-Star, go!"

Murray checked Melanie against a support beam, smashing her head against it. She slipped to the linoleum. He stomped her with listing fury until he slipped on brain leaking from nostrils and collapsed beside her. He laughed in a rush of triumph and relief.

Smith, now smoking a joint, slow-clapped.

Hodgepodge was displeased. "I'm sorry, Officer Smith. Are we boring you?"

Actually, yeah. "I was hoping somebody was at least gonna hit the pretty one before the finale."

Murray scrambled to his feet, looking for his medal. Hodgepodge smiled and summoned him with a head tip. Murray joined him, a minion to be admitted to the fold. He alerted to something, drew closer, and sniffed Hodgepodge.

Hodgepodge offered a knowing look. "Do you like that?"

"Yeah."

"They let me grow mint leaves in my cell. I mash them in water and splash it onto my face after shaving. It's quite refreshing, actually."

Hodgepodge looked at me. I frowned. "The only reason they'd buy it is because you're infamous, and you're infamous because you murdered all those people. The victims will get the proceeds."

He sighed. "Again, American parochiality thwarts my genius."

He pulled Murray closer. "Right, All-Star?"

"Right."

"I'm so proud of you."

The chains and shackles fell away easily, never having been locked. They dropped to the floor, clanging, heralding a glorious return to form. Murray marvelled.

"My beautiful boy."

Like I mentioned, Hodgepodge is hunky strong. He broke Murray's neck smoothly. Murray felt nothing but the joy of belonging.

It was probably the closest thing to euthanasia Hodgepodge ever practiced.

***

Smith left us to the spend the bonus money I gave him. Hodgepodge and I drank champagne while reclining on sour mattresses someone should have long ago burned. He wore only the Hodgepodge hoodie he'd taken from Murray after dispatching him.

I held up my glass. "Happy birthday, darling. Here's to extra credit."

We clinked and drained the glasses.

Then we kissed.

EASTER EGGS FOR CHRISTMAS

The movie was called *Sweet Christmas*, and it made me want to kill myself. It was one of many holiday-themed films Heritage Studios produced to ensure wall-to-wall Christmas hell from Thanksgiving till New Year's, films re-affirming anodyne Norman Rockwell people in their anodyne Norman Rockwell-ness.

And, of course, my girlfriend Patience loved them. "You're not watching! It's the best part!"

A Christmas Miracle is about Delilah, a single mom who hooks up with Colton, her former high school flame, after both return to Wisconsin for Christmas. Both are divorced, and both have kids (Delilah has a daughter, Colton a son). And Delilah's still hot for Colton, but her ex is an insufferable soft-rock light-beer douchebag so she's reluctant to retry romance. Then her mom collapses and offers a Wisdom for Life soliloquy from her hospital bed.

"Honey, you've got to live your life."

"What do you mean?"

"You know what I mean. You can't live in fear of making mistakes. Love is worth mistakes. And I don't think Colton is a mistake."

"Mom, let's just concentrate on getting you better."

"No. Listen to me. I know how much Campbell hurt you. And I know that you never want to risk your heart again. But that's what life is about. Risking your heart. If you're not risking your heart, you're dying a little bit inside, every day."

Delilah sobs.

"Sweetie. Go to him. Go make candy together. And babies. Lots of babies!"

Delilah smiles awkwardly. So does Marla, her daughter.

It was all pure boner death. Delilah goes to Colton, who's behind on filling a massive Christmas order at his family's candy company. She offers to help, he accepts, and the candy cane goes into the fudge. I wish.

Patience clung to me. I tried clinging back. She slapped away my hand.

***

At the next commercial break, Patience went to the bathroom.

I texted my friend Brody:

Me: "Dude, chickflicking w/P-. The Heritage Studios Channel."

Brody: Nelson from *The Simpsons* "Ha-ha" emoticon.

Me: Middle finger GIF.

Brody: Cat emoticon, bullwhip emoticon.

Me: "LOL"

Brody: "Dude, check this out:"

He sent a link to a *Reddit* thread discussing hidden satanic content in Heritage films:

"Dude, I heard that there was a post-production tech at Heritage Studios who said all the family friendly bullshit was just a cover and the whole enterprise is pure Satan. Supposedly there are Easter egg incantations encrypted in the dialogue of some of their Christmas movies and, if you play them in the right sequence, they'll summon a demon. The movies are *Sweet Christmas*, *A Christmas Miracle*, and *Christmas Reunion*. He said to look for the cheesiest money shot line from each film's climax. I don't know what order to use, but there aren't that many combinations so I guess it won't take long to figure it out."

Me: "I'm totally doing this!"

Brody: "Me 2!"

"George! Oh my God!"

I looked up. Patience was pissed.

"What? It's the commercials."

I pocketed the phone. Next up was *A Christmas Miracle*. It was about some kid who needs a kidney transplant and the only donor is a guy who hates kids because they remind him of his son who died at Christmas. Cheap irony for cheaper tears. At least I could watch for the satanic money quotes. After a hundred minutes of me wanting to fuck a belt sander, it climaxed.

Mr. Crowley, teary-eyed, held the boy's hand in the hospital bed. "Mr. Crowley?"

"I'm here."

"You came."

Mr. Crowley smiles. "You remind me a lot of Charlie. He had spunk. Just like you. And he was persistent. Just like you. And I know he'd want me to help you. He'd want me to be the best guy I can be. And I want to be the best guy I can be. For him. For you. For me. I mean, if we can't love each other, we're hopeless."

Mr. Crowley pulls up a chair. "I guess what I'm trying to say is, well, I've got an extra kidney, and I heard you need one."

"Really?!"

"Really."

"Wow! Thanks, Mr. Crowley! This is the best Christmas ever!"

"And, maybe after we're better, we can throw the football around a little. If you like."

The boy opens his arms. Mr. Crowley leans in and hugs him while the boy's mother sobs in delight.

I mean, if we can't love each other, we're hopeless. That had to be it.

***

Christmas Reunion was up next. It's about Branson, another spunky kid who hopes to unite his town's acridly divided residents by orchestrating a Christmas parade. Things turn unexpectedly delightful when—wait for it—the kid collapses at the post-parade party because inoperable brain tumour. I guess I'd have seen it coming if I hadn't zoned the first act. Anyway, the climax: Another hospital room. Another wrenching exchange. Branson's brain dead.

The formerly warring townsfolk stand before his bed, weepy.

"Why didn't you tell us?"

"He didn't want you to know. He wanted it to be authentic. The coming together. The making peace. He knew that if everybody knew he was dying, it wouldn't be real. He said, 'Mommy, if they don't change inside, none of it matters.' Looks like you did."

The townsfolk join hands and sang *Away in a Manger* as the doctors come for Tommy's organs. Coming for his organs was extra creepy, but the Heritage folks want to make sure we understand how important organ donation is.

It had to be the Mommy line.

***

Patience recorded the movies, so I copied the money shot quotes from each one and synced them with a computer in every possible permutation. I guessed that the "risking your heart" line from *Sweet Christmas* was the other quote. This order cheesed most: "'If you're not risking your heart, you're dying a little bit inside, every day.' 'Mommy, if they don't change inside, none of it matters.' 'I mean, if we can't love each other, we're hopeless.'"

Nothing happened. No inverted pentagram of fire, no bathing in blood, no orgy of unspeakable horrors. Bah, humbug.

***

Saturday morning came. Patience was on the couch, coffee in hand, bingeing afresh. I settled down beside her. She smiled and curled into me.

"What's this one?"

"*The Christmas Palace*. It's about divorcees who bond while coordinating their town's life-sized gingerbread Christmas village."

It was unexpectedly moving. I mean, it was formulaic, and you knew that there'd be a happy ending (if it was to be bittersweet like *The Christmas Parade* then the dying character's illness would be disclosed at the first plot point). But, instead of hating, I surrendered to it. It was warm and beige and life-affirming.

We spent the morning on the couch, except for when I made Patience breakfast: fresh blueberry muffins and coddled eggs on rosemary turkey red bliss potato hash.

"Wow. I didn't know you baked. What prompted all this?"

I kissed her forehead. "Because you're awesome."

Afternoon brought *Undivorced for Christmas*, *Hidden Angels*, and *Home for Christmas*. There was something reassuring about the monotony of it all, like a liturgy. In *Home for Christmas*, by far the best, retirement home and orphanage directors find romance while arranging a retiree/orphan Christmas shindig.

The climax illuminated love's power to free us from ourselves. It involved Billy, a boy who hadn't spoken since his parents died, and Mr. Chambers, a retired baseball coach who hadn't spoken since his children left him at the home. Throughout the film, Billy did nothing but throw a baseball into his glove, more vigorously if he was angry. And Mr. Chambers did nothing but watch baseball games on television, always alone.

During the party, Billy sits in a corner, balling the glove while glumly beholding the proceedings. Mr. Chambers approaches him. "That's a nice glove."

Billy looks up, half-spooked, half-delighted.

Sam, the rest home director, and Sally, the orphanage director, watch in delighted anticipation.

"Mind if I take a look?"

Billy hesitates. Then he hands Mr. Chambers the glove, however tentatively. But he keeps the ball.

Mr. Chambers smiles. "Glove ain't no good without the ball."

Billy hesitates, then gives him the ball.

Mr. Chambers dons the glove and, with emerging enthusiasm, throws the ball into it several times. "Yeah, first class all the way!"

"My dad gave it to me. He said that, if I practiced enough, it would become part of my hand."

"Your poppy was a smart, smart man."

My phone buzzed.

"George!" Patience dabbed tears with a tissue.

"I know. I know."

I glanced at the message. It was Brody.

Brody: "Did U try?"

Me: "Y"

Brody: "Blastoff??"

Me: "N"

Brody: "Me neither."

Patience took the phone and put it on a table beside her.

I smiled. "Sorry."

We kissed.

***

I was delighted when I saw it. I'm not sure how they got my e-mail address. Maybe from the TV service. It was an invitation to a Heritage Studios meet and greet on Sunday afternoon. When I showed Patience, she almost fainted with excitement.

"Oh my God it's at the Blackwatch. Oh. My. God. Theyevenhaveadresscode.Mr.Chamberswillbethere! OhmyGodohmyGodohmyGodcanwepleasego?!"

I smiled noncommittally.

"Eeeeaahhh! We're going, right? Please? Right?"

I feigned reluctance. "It's one of the last regular season games tomorrow."

Then I smiled before the disappointment could reach her face. "Of course we're going."

We kissed. She didn't slap my hand away.

***

It was first class all the way. The stars of all the films we'd watched were there. They even handed out autographed vanity shots, no charge. Patience went to the line for Chauncey Bellemoor, the actor who played Mr. Chambers in *Home for Christmas*. I went to the bar to get us drinks.

I was only mildly surprised to see Brody.

"Brodester."

"Hey."

"Where's Lila?" Lila was Brody's girlfriend.

"She's getting the autograph of that guy who played Mr. Chambers in—"

"*Home for Christmas*. Dude, it's the best one."

"I know." He held up a baseball and glove. "Think he'll sign them?"

"Dude, it's Mr. Chambers. What do you think?"

"Are you going to the Q and A?"

"Of course."

We got some sparkling cider.

I raised my glass. "To Mr. Chambers."

"Mr. Chambers."

We clinked our glasses.

***

The Grand Ballroom overflowed. Brody let me admire the autographed ball and glove, but only after he put them in mylar bags. Patience and Lily stood in front of us. The applause shook the room when Jeremiah Androos, Heritage's CEO, jogged onto the dais. His stars rose and flanked him like an honour guard.

Jeremiah stood before the podium, greying and avuncular, twice as charming as Mr. Chambers. I envied Patience because she could have his baby. "Bless you, bless you all. And thank you for coming. Without you and your commitment to Heritage, the Lord wouldn't have made us what we have become."

He closed his eyes. "Now, let us pray."

We bowed our heads.

He continued. "'If you're not risking your heart, you're dying a little bit inside, every day.' 'Mommy, if they don't change inside, none of it matters.' 'I mean, if we can't love each other, we're hopeless.'"

A blessed calm welled within me. Brody and I hugged. We were brothers forever.

Patience's blood was warm and soothing as it drenched me. The knife was surgically sharp and glided through her throat. Brody bled Lily the same way. We high fived while guiding them to the ballroom floor so they could die without injuring themselves.

I looked around and discovered that every other guy in the room did the same.

We looked up in unison at the dais when someone thumped the microphone. Jeremiah had these wonderfully black eyes. So did the actors.

I smiled at Brody. "You ready?"

He nodded.

We slashed our throats together, then fell in unison with the others, a beautiful symmetry. We died smiling.

It was a Christmas miracle. From Hell.

THE ICE CREAM MAN

I'm the ice cream man. I sell chemically engineered, dairy-free frozen treats Congress calls "ice cream" because Big Agra's lobbyists pay them to, which makes it totally legal, if scandalous. On the up side, I'm giving children smiles; on the down, I'm probably giving their children autism.

It's a great job. I got it today. It won't last long, and that's probably for the best.

***

I didn't plan the killings. They just kind of happened. I have Obsessive Compulsive Disorder. OCD: Your brain throttles you with constant fears often unrealistic and then demands you follow rituals to abate them, a loop of worries and remedies prompting more worries and remedies, horror undiminished by monotony, and the things you fear are more likely to bedevil you the less likely they are to occur. It comes from wanting to abolish uncertainty, or from not being able to be God but not letting that stop you from trying.

Managing the fears, putting them away to make way for new ones, is like playing *Tetris*. You know, the video game where you manipulate falling shapes of varying configurations to fit together into solid lines which then disappear. But victory invites inevitable defeat: Every time you create an imperfect line, it stays, crowding the field of play from the bottom up and giving you fewer opportunities for mistakes. The imperfect lines accumulate till there's no more room and it's game over.

Over the years, I've gotten used to the shapes: Things move but seem to stay put.

For instance, I know the government's coming for me. The fact that they haven't proves nothing. Still, I follow rules scrupulously. That way, whatever hedge-fund-law-school-educated attorney the state appoints to lose my case will have to ignore the obvious to do so. But the more I do to avoid getting got, the more suspicious I look. I mean, everybody has a smart phone. Except me. It's basically a surveillance device (not that I get out much). No social media presence, either. Which looks creepy, like I'm hiding something. But I just can't.

And then there are other people, whom I avoid. They're risky. Dr. Simon says isolation makes me sicker. Who knows, maybe I'll fall and starve to death in my kitchen. I'd get one of those medical alert devices, but EMTs work for the government, and they don't need a warrant when you invite them in.

I'm not completely isolated. I talk to the postman every day. Assuming it's Mitch. Otherwise I just wait for the him to leave and grab the mail. I also waive at my neighbour, Roberta. She's nice enough. Invasive sometimes, bringing over chocolate chip cookies and trying to chat me up. Probably wants to mix fluids. Probably has hepatitis slow burning into full blown liver cancer or something else no amount of latex will guard against.

I don't eat the cookies. Not that I think Roberta wants to poison me. But they might include some unknown allergen and I wouldn't be able to get to the epi pens in time. So, I toss them. I mean, I could feed them to the birds, but then I might accidentally poison Chauncey, the neighbourhood's roving retriever, and—boom—prison. You know what they do to animal abusers in prison? Makes you wish you were a kiddie raper instead. Not that I wish I was. Please don't think that. It was only an example.

Anyway, like I said, the killings just kind of happened. I work from home as a freelance quality assurance tester. I review mundane things like breakfast cereals and desk lamps. For example, Notes of Oats is really yummy. And its composition makes it unlikely to convey salmonella or some other pathogen. In case you wondered.

Product testers get lots of mail. That's why Mitch knows me so well. He asks questions that make me uncomfortable, even though everything I do is one hundred percent legal.

I expected questions when he came to the door this morning bearing the usual armful of packages, and I greeted him wearing my usual germ mask. And so began our litany.

He smiled. "Still not dead."

"Well, on paper, at least."

"What are you testing today?"

"Cleaning products."

"That sounds terribly appropriate."

"What do you mean?"

"I mean, you obviously care a lot about cleanliness."

"And you don't?"

"Or you're just tidying up the mass grave in your basement. Or is it your freezer?"

I looked from side to side nervously. "Really, I'm not."

"You sure?" He smiled.

"Really."

Was he kidding? "Mass grave in the basement" is an old joke, ever since Gacy. And please don't judge me for referring to him by his last name. Everybody refers to Gacy by his last name. Like Bundy. And Manson. But, strangely, not Ed Gein.

How well did I really know Mitch? Maybe he was in witness protection. They work at the Post Office, right? No, that didn't make sense. WitSec wouldn't put him in front of so many people. But they could put him in the back where they scan and photograph everybody's mail. And don't tell me they don't.

Maybe he's surveilling me. And he doesn't show up every day because that would look strange. Maybe they think I'm a pervert. Or serial killer. But I'm not. Really. Or, at least, I wasn't. I guess I'm a spree killer. Not sure there's a huge difference. Except I'm more likely to get grouped with mass shooters, and therefore violated in prison. But I'm not a pervert.

***

I try some "ice cream." It's a brittle cone with phony vanilla and an allegedly chocolate topping. Food science is an abomination that just invents tasty new ways to give everybody cancer. Like the supposedly safe insecticides they spray everywhere, or those artificial sweeteners that don't kill lab rats quickly enough for anybody to worry. But it is yummy. My therapist would be pleased. Normally, I don't eat anything containing preservatives. Notes of Oats are organic, by the way, in case you wondered.

***

The knife slipped in effortlessly. I practiced many times in the mirror. I bought the self-defence book second hand because the FBI monitors Amazon purchases. I got the knife for cash at an army-navy store. The book didn't mention containing blood loss, but I figured I should avoid major arteries. Splashed blood's a poor pathogen vector, but, hey, c'mon, it's me. Who knows what Mitch caught before witness protection? Maybe that's why he entered. Free healthcare.

Straight into the eye. Eight inches. Pretty much instant death. He shuddered finally in my arms as I dragged him inside.

I guided him into the plastic on the floor. Not that I'd planned to murder anyone, but I knew that if I ever had to the jury would convict. *He's so weird. Of course he did it.*

I wrapped him, unexpectedly thankful that Mom insisted I learn the art of gift wrapping. I even won the third-grade wrapping competition. Mom had the certificate framed; It adorns my study.

Mom loved me. Probably too much. I was always pristine. Perfectly groomed. But never free. She spoke in aphorisms that haunt me: "Death is in the details!"; "Put everything in its proper place and you'll always have a smiling face!"; and "When you kiss somebody you kiss everyone they ever kissed, and everyone they ever kissed ever kissed!" She stopped kissing my father shortly after I was born. Surprise, I'm an only child.

***

But what about the mail?

My house can't be Mitch's last stop. I mean, there's your probable cause. *Besides, the guy who lives there gives me a ferret-hoarder vibe. Those poor creatures.* Not that that mattered since conservative Supreme Court appointees neutralized the warrant requirement. Not that they would have found anything. Till today, at least. But who says they won't pre-crime you by planting dope and— boom—prison.

I dragged Mitch, who is thankfully slight, into my bedroom and undressed him. I promise I obtained no illicit pleasures from doing so. The uniform fit. Even the shoes.

The mail in the bag covered my street and several adjoining streets. How far to deter suspicion? I guessed my street and at least two more. Roughly fifty houses.

New fears loomed. I froze up: What if people expecting Mitch see me instead? Odds are, some retiree with too little to do and too much to say will interrupt me. Or someone will notice I'm not Mitch. *Why yes officer, since you mention it, it wasn't Mitch. It was someone I'd never seen before. Would you like to see my private surveillance footage? I mean, I know it's a little paranoid, but you never know, right?*

And should I wear the germ mask? *Why is the postman wearing that mask? Does he know something we don't? Maybe we should call the Post Office and complain. Maybe he's a terrorist. Americans can be terrorists, too.*

I looked at my watch. Two-thirty. School was getting out. It was now or never. I donned rubber gloves to prevent fingerprints. Then—wait, what am I thinking? I could just reclaim the neighbours' mail and say mine never arrived. Sid works till eight. He lives alone. Same with Lucy. Two or three minutes, max—

My doorbell RANG.

I looked at the security monitor by the door hooked to the camera on the porch. It was my other neighbour, Roberta. Maybe she'd go away.

She rang again.

"Hello? Mr. Buckley? I saw Mitch and wondered where he went. My catheter package is past due and, well, I'm sorry to be a pest—"

I opened the door.

She froze. "You work for the Post Office?"

"Just started."

Same knife, same eye. I swear I hadn't done this before. Well, only once.

Briefly I worried about giving her Mitch's diseases, since I didn't sterilize the blade. Then I laughed uncomfortably. After this is all over, I'll have to bleach the knife and bake it at five hundred—no, it's going in the ocean, pronto. I wonder if I can get it there without getting searched. I mean, it's only a knife. It's not illegal. *So, why the knife? It's not illegal, Officer. I know, but what, are you afraid of something? Why so nervous?* Then, suddenly, I've killed again. Ugh.

***

Mom notices my belt is unbuckled. She slaps me. "I told you! Little things! They add up! They'll kill you!"

I cry. She slaps me again. Blood flecks the adjacent wall.

***

Roberta snuggled Mitch. I had plenty of plastic to wrap them both. I sighed. Then I went to undeliver the mail. I slipped outside. Sunny, quiet. No one in sight. I took a deep breath, then removed the mask. Mitch's shoes were really comfy, even with two pairs of socks and plastic bags on because Mitch's cleanliness crack probably meant he had toe fungus. I thought about wearing my own shoes. Then I thought better of it. *You know officer, the postman had new shoes. I mean, maybe it's nothing, but you might want to get a plaster cast and compare it with people's shoes in the neighbourhood. I mean, you just never know, right? Good idea, ma'am.*

Sid's mail was still there. I snagged it, put it back in the bag, and moved quickly to Lucy. Also there. Sigh of relief, snagged, bagged, easy-peasy. I feel compelled to mention that mail theft is a federal offense warranting up to five years in prison and a $250,000 fine. At least last I checked. Not that I'd, well...

I turned back to my house. Oh, happy day! There was an ice cream truck parked in Roberta's drive. The ice cream man, in his clinically white uniform, slipped out the driver's side and onto her porch. Her door was open.

"Robbie? Robbie?"

I approached my door and waited, hoping he wouldn't notice. Then I figured that if I didn't deliver the mail, he'd be like, *"Why is the postman creeping on that guy's porch? Is he some kind of pervert? Maybe I should call the police. Or at least take a picture."* I pretended to deliver my mail, hoping he'd leave. He didn't. Instead, he approached me.

***

Mom slaps me again. Then there's this wet crunch and her blood flecks my face. She drops to the floor, shuddering. There's Dad, wielding the baseball bat I never used because *"Do you want him to end up in a wheelchair?"*

He hits her still. Then he drops the bat and hugs me. His expression mixes elation and agony.

"Let's get sushi."

"Huh?"

"C'mon, you'll love it."

"Mom said we'll get parasites."

"That's exactly why we're getting it, boy. Time to stretch your boundaries."

"Can we get ice cream?"

"We're getting sushi."

"Please?"

***

The ice cream guy accosted me. I instantly distrusted him.

"Hey, you seen Roberta Parker today? Her door's open, so she can't have gone far."

I froze in horror. Then, as I always knew I would, I confessed: "She's in my bedroom."

His face fell. "What do you mean?"

"She's in my bedroom."

Rage took him. He entered without even asking. This day was never going to end.

I followed him, grabbing the baseball bat I kept just inside the door. His skull cracked, and he dropped to the floor. I put him beside Roberta. Another perfect fit. And still plenty of plastic wrap remained.

I sat on the bed and took stock. An ice cream truck idled in the drive and soon kids would swarm, looking for the ice cream man killed for having the wrong girlfriend. Plus, some super-officious neighbour fretting global warming was destined to complain about the exhaust. I sighed, knowing what I had to do.

Hat aside, his uniform was unbloodied. And, because fortune blessed me with an average weight and build, it fit. I declined to worry over the shoes this time, probably because all the other concerns had crowded them out. Besides, I probably didn't need to leave the truck.

I rolled out a few blocks before I put the music on. It was like my product, sweet, soulless, fake. I pondered being a postman or ice cream man, roving suburbia in an endless loop of banal horror, time dissolving into monotony doing a job never done.

On the plus side, Dr. Simon would approve. Ice cream man is exactly the kind of job he suggested: easily mastered routines affording constant socialization. Plus, everybody's happy to see me. They can't wait to play chicken with hyperglycaemia. And crazy retirees who chase ice cream trucks with shotguns for disturbing their midday siestas are statistically unlikely at best.

***

I win: ice cream instead of sushi. Dad fidgets while I eat.

"Perce, your mom was usually right. She was a planner, and better than me at life. I'm thinking you're a planner, too."

Our booth's window faces the parking lot where people swarm our car. Mom's in the back seat, her head misshapen from batting practice. Incoming sirens wail.

Suddenly, Dad has a gun. He splatters onto the window, my sundae, and me. I'm still eating when cops come. It never occurs to me to stop.

***

"Dr. Simon?"

"Percival? Is everything okay?"

"Yes and no."

"What does that mean?"

"I've made some . . . breakthroughs. I'm sitting in a truck about a mile from my house. I'm selling ice cream. I feel . . . kinda great. I'm out of the house, in the sunshine, eating a chocolate vanilla cone. It's fake, but yummy. I'm a kid again."

"Percival, that's wonderful! I'm so happy for you! Wait—What's that in the background?"

"Those are sirens."

"Is everything okay?"

"Well, like I said, yes and no."

***

They found me by finding Mitch. In my haste to deliver the mail, I forgot his cell phone. Rookie mistake. Well, I guess I am a rookie, no matter how many pre-emptive homicides I've imagined. They tracked it and found him slowly freezing in the back of the truck next to the Vanilla Surprise and Mint Madness. It was in the uniform I'd put back on him because if they found him without it they'd call me a pervert, and you know what happens to perverts in prison.

Luckily, the ice cream man had sold most of his inventory and hadn't re-stocked. There was ample room for him, Roberta, and Mitch. Another perfect fit. The cold kept them fresh for the CSIs. I wonder if they told the kids about them. I mean, the chances of contamination were so minor that they'd only bother someone like me. Which is why I ate from the freezer on the other side of the truck.

Getting the bodies in was easier than I anticipated. It helped that nobody questions the ice cream man. Even though they should. Even though he's hawking poison happiness wrapped in plastic that causes autism.

And not just because, at least for a few hours today, he's me.

ARS GRATIA MORTIS

Fame can be poison, but I still can't get enough. I'm Stormy Stillwater, and I host *TRENDER!* It's a feel-good variety talk show in daytime syndication watched mostly by retirees and the professionally unemployed. I've interviewed almost every celebrity worth interviewing, along with countless child prodigies, maimed achievers, and absurd philanthropists. I'm a household name, the face of pabulum programming.

But I'm only as memorable as my last gig, which is one of the reasons the bastards were replacing me. No one knew it yet. I didn't know it, really. I just suspected. Normally, my renewal negotiations started months before contract expiration. My contract expired in two months, and I'd heard nothing. My agent didn't seem perturbed, but he was a survivor. If he wanted to continue to work with my production company's mega parent, he would likely bullshit me till it was too late.

So, at fifty-five, it was off to the knackery. Maybe I could hawk infomercial impotence solutions or sell riverfront chateaus in Arkansas. Maybe I could snuff it by driving my Porsche off a cliff and be remembered fondly as one of those "gone too soon." Or maybe, just maybe, I could be transubstantiated into a cultural icon forever memed and merched.

***

We sat on the *TRENDER!* dais, minimalist cool with black leather chairs and a brushed steel table between us. I'd put a human skull rendered in crystal on the table tonight as a grim welcome to the guest, Excalibur Smith. He was only thirty and already the world's most famous and infamous performance artist. He wore a double-breasted white suit. Colourful tattoos covered his (shaven) head and hands. I wore all black. An ironic contrast, perhaps. Behind us loomed a massive monitor with "*TRENDER!*" onscreen.

The studio audience hummed. Half hated Smith. My producers had combed the weirder segments of social media to find religious fundamentalists to come and revile. He was a murderer, after all. The other half were the usual randoms and tourists looking for a semi-religious life experience.

I smiled a plastic smile. "Good evening and welcome to *TRENDER!*, your first and last word on what matters. I'm your host, Stormy Stillwater. Tonight, we're discussing Omegamania, the latest euthanasia craze among the rich and famous. With us is its creator, Excalibur Smith."

Smith was serious. I think smiling was beneath him. Onscreen behind us footage played on one of his works. In it, an elegant old guy wearing a pith helmet and gaudy lifejacket smiled from within a giant, wood-fired cauldron. It sat in a jungle clearing adjacent grass huts. Colourfully painted, barely dressed natives tossed fruit into the cauldron. Another, wearing a headdress adorned with three human skulls, stirred the pot. Excalibur posed with an arm around the skull-hatted chef.

"Who's this guy?"

"That's Malcolm Stills. He was a huge environmentalist and wanted to die sustainably while supporting an underappreciated culture. We found a tribe in Asia still practicing cannibalism and consulted several anthropologists about how best to approach them. We employed maximal cultural contamination precautions while still allowing Mr. Stills his sustainable death. A win on all fronts."

From the audience, boos subdued tepid applause.

"Your appearance won us scores of death threats. In fact, oddsmakers think someone will kill you during this episode. Are you concerned?"

Excalibur seemed almost affronted, but bravado smoothed his response. "No. I slaughter sacred cows, so of course the small-minded hate me."

More boos. New footage appeared on the screen. It depicted a gigantic ant farm. Feeding the ants was a middle-aged woman's corpse, half-submerged in the farm's soil. Her expression was perverse joy. Excalibur stood atop the soil, pouring honey on the woman's face.

Excalibur continued. "It's pitiable, really. Don't hate the tiger for being a tiger. Be honoured when he eats you."

"How modest."

"Modesty is for slaves of the petit bourgeois order."

The feed changed again, this time depicting an old woman, wearing pearls and holding a precious, petite dog. They had the same fussy expression.

"Well then, tell me about Omegamania."

"I was having tea with billionaire arms heiress and philanthropist Lizzie Cairns. Lizzie confided she had anal cancer and wanted to die meaningfully, not surrounded by Matisse prints in some cosy, Eurotrash suicide hutch."

On screen appeared a lavish, high-concept museum atrium. A sombrely suited, bland-faced ticket taker behind a marble kiosk pointed white-gloved hands at signs advertising two admission options. The first read: "Admission: $250 per person." The second: "Make a mortal choice." Below the second sign, a video monitor depicted a caged, white rat sniffing the air. Gas jets flanked the rat. Patrons stood transfixed before the monitor. The whole thing was terribly meta, people watching monitored people watching monitored people watching a monitored rat.

"I'd just debuted *Mortal Choices* at the Manhattan Museum. It was an installation exhibit allowing patrons to choose between paying regular admission and pushing a button that might kill a rat caged inside. The animal rights people objected, but Lizzy's lawyers got a court order allowing the exhibition to continue on free speech grounds."

On screen, an obese, too eager boy pushed the button.

"Might kill the rat?"

"Pushing the button didn't always dispense the gas. Sometimes it closed the circuit, and sometimes it didn't. This uncertainty helped people to rationalize pushing the button. Oh, in case you're worried, we used a fast-acting nerve gas. It was all quite humane."

Behind us, Lizzie Cairns wore a black evening gown and restraints at her wrists and ankles, anchored in velour cushions.

"I decided to extend the *Mortal Choices* paradigm to Lizzie's piece. The button fired a minor calibre gun moving back and forth on a rail before her."

The gun fired.

"Those pushing the button didn't know the gun's position, just as the Mortal Choosers didn't know if they were gassing the rat. Call it my little homage to Schrödinger's Cat."

The bullet just missed Lizzie's torso. Her face was all terror and exhilaration.

"It took almost two hundred shots before Lizzie departed us. She died a hero."

He beamed. The audience booed.

"A hero?"

"Indeed. She died for art. For what worthier cause may one die?"

An image of Excalibur on the cover of *For Art's Sake* magazine appeared. He tango-posed with a skeleton. There was a long-stemmed rose in its teeth. The caption: "Excalibur Smith: Knockin' 'Em Dead!"

"In any event, after Lizzie, things took off."

"Yes. Suddenly, I had more clients than I could reasonably accept without being vulgar."

An image of Excalibur on the cover of *Park Slope Snooper* appeared, showing him surrounded by oddball assistants holding tablet computers and file folders. The caption: "Through the Eye of the Needle: Choosing Excalibur Smith's Omegamaniacs."

"I devised an interview process. So many tears. One dowager said she would die if I didn't kill her. Rejected."

The audience chuckled. Excalibur at last was charming them.

"I'm sure you declined some worthy candidates."

"No. Sponges all. Ironically, their suicides would be a public service. But I'm not a bus."

Behind us appeared my reply: Excalibur mugged with a cadaverous boy in a hospital bed. Both offered a thumbs-up. "Oh, come now. What about Billy Billingsley?"

Video played showing Excalibur tossing a terrified Billy out the back of a high-flying airplane. Billy wore a bomb vest.

"Right. Billy was five, dying of ALS, and wanted, in his words, 'to live in the sky.' I gave him that. Pro bono."

On screen, Excalibur, tears in his eyes, triggers a remote detonator. "He had a voyager's soul."

The audience cooed. Skyborne kiddie demolitions were awesome TV.

Suddenly, I couldn't wait any longer. "And I don't?"

The audience WOOOOed. Excalibur, beaming, brough a tablet from beneath his jacket and read aloud from it. "'I want Excalibur to dispatch me while I interview him on *TRENDER!*. My ratings are in retreat and I don't want to end up absorbed by mediocrity.'"

"You bastard!" I pointed a pistol at him. It was a .357 magnum with hollow point bullets. I was told that the calibre at that range with those bullets meant instant death. I figured if I was going to off myself, I wouldn't want to half-ass it and end up a quad in a sip-n-puff chair.

Excalibur kept cool.

"I demand you kill me!"

The audience froze.

"No."

They cheered.

"Coercion spoils creative integrity. Besides, no credible curator would include you in my catalogue. You'd be some kind of asterisk, a curiosity, a game show trivia question."

And then something wonderful happened. Excalibur extended his hand. "C'mon. You don't want your legacy to be an asterisk."

Then came the tears. Mine, mostly. Flooding forth, all my middle-aged angst and anonymity terrors overcoming me. I gave him the gun. "I'm so sorry."

At last, a smile. "No worries, Stormy."

He fired, point blank range. Chunks of me splattered the set decorations, which I imagined would fetch thousands at auction. Especially the skull.

"Go with God."

The audience offered a standing ovation while Excalibur bowed. Immortality was mine.

FRIENDS IN THE END

The house was a quiet bungalow in the Cleveland suburbs, familiar to me since childhood, good memories abruptly turning bad.

The family smiled when I arrived: Mom, five-year-old Billy, and eleven-year-old Hannah. "Oh, thank you for coming. It's worse than ever."

I regarded them calmly. "Are you all out?"

"Yes."

"Don't you have another daughter? Kendall, right?"

"She's got a class downtown."

"Okay."

Hannah spoke up. "Did you tell him about bleeding walls? And the endless screaming?"

"Yes. It'll be okay." Then I regarded Mom gravely. "Don't come back in till I say so. Do you understand?"

She nodded with matching gravity. I put a hand on her shoulder. She smiled weakly.

I entered the house.

***

It had been awhile. Liddell (Liddy for short) seemed terribly happy. "How've you been, Jonesy? Or, should I say, Father Jones."

I touched my collar almost by instinct.

"I never figured you for the priesthood."

"I never figured a lot of things, Liddy."

"Can't argue that."

I looked around the parlour. It hadn't changed much. Same white plaster with mahogany accents. Upper-middle class Shangri-La, circa 1920.

"I'm really glad you're here."

"Me too, notwithstanding the circumstances."

"Notwithstanding the circumstances?"

"Your campaign of terror against our friends outside."

"Ah, screw them. If you knew half of what I know about them, you wouldn't be here. Plus, God they're dumb. I mean, sterilize-as-a-public-service dumb."

"They're God's children."

"*They're God children.* So are all the chickens they eat in nugget form."

He regarded the pigskin bag at my right. "Are we gonna talk about Jesus? Do some Bible study?"

"Would you like to?"

"What do you think?"

I smiled involuntarily.

***

Twenty years ago, Liddy and I were thirteen and best friends. I was bookish, bored by sports. He was better-adjusted, attractive to girls. Saturday afternoons, we'd explore abandoned houses, look for dead animals, and wade in the local creek. We were pretty far from Jesus. But not from Satan.

The local library's occult collection, once forgotten, became news after a fundamentalist pastor decried its presence and ready accessibility to minors. Moral crusaders, immune to irony, forget that the quickest way to interest adolescent boys in something—anything—is to try to forbid it. Liddy and I borrowed the whole collection. Among them were Crowley's *The Book of the Law* and *Key of Solomon*, LaVey's *Satanic Bible*, various grimoires, and even the *Malleus Maleficarum*. All that Latin I'd learned at St. Agatha's grammar school finally mattered.

***

"Bleeding walls, huh?"
Liddy smiled. "Bitchin', if not original."
I smiled. "Remember that creepy undertaker?"

***

One spell demanded human remains. Something about affording a demonic entity carnal purchase in this world. So, one night we stole Liddy's mom's hospital pass (she was a nurse) and snuck into the morgue. We figured it would be empty (at least of the living) and we could get our special ingredient.

We found a gnarly accident victim still bagged on a gurney. I grabbed a hacksaw from an instrument tray. Liddy held his arm. I was about to cut, then paused.

"Hurry up!"
"We have to respect the dead."
"Really!?"

I took a deep breath.

"Hey kids."

We froze.

"Whatcha doin'?"

We were too terrified to look. It was the coroner. He had a loopy smile and blood-stained scrubs. He smiled like he'd just gotten lucky. I'm pretty sure he was tripping. He tossed us a box of latex gloves. "Remember! Always use protection!"

Looking back, a bent coroner was a pretty obvious omen of our fate.

***

"I still can't believe it worked."

"Neither can I."

"I mean, it really worked. Well, not exactly how we wanted. I mean, well, you know what I mean. But it worked."

I felt for the crucifix in my waistcoat pocket. "I know. It's one of the reasons—"

"You went over to the dark side."

I frowned. "C'mon, Liddy. Really?"

"Well, what do you want me to say?"

***

We drew the pentagram on the basement floor in kosher salt. We used black candles for light because it was cool. Liddy put the arm in the pentagram's centre;

I uttered the incantations. Liddy stifled laughter while he watched. Neither of us expected anything to happen, like when we played that old Mötley Crüe album backwards to hear satanic messages.

Nothing did. Then, without warning, the air felt alive. And wrong.

***

"I thought it was pretty sweet."

"Of course you did. You were a thirteen-year-old boy."

"C'mon. It was pretty sweet."

I grimaced.

"You're smiling on the inside. Whatever you say, I know it. I know you."

"You knew me twenty years ago."

"I still know you. You can hide behind Jesus all you like; I know you thought it was goddamned magnificent."

***

The demon didn't look like a demon at all. It looked like a soft, middle-aged guy doomed to an HR career. We didn't know what to make of him.

He smiled, then held his hands up in an almost menacing pose.

We laughed nervously.

"What the hell are you?"

"I'm Astaroth."

"You don't look like an Astaroth."

"Oh, right. You thought I'd be so unspeakably terrifying as permanently to disfigure your psyche? Well, the meat you chose to make me came from a nobody whose idea of daring is getting two desserts at the mega buffet. Garbage in, garbage out."

I regarded Liddy with triumphal contempt. "I told you it mattered. But no, you said we were conjuring a demon and a demon's a demon's a demon."

Astaroth smiled. "Well, you're both right. I mean, if I looked like some A-list hotness, you'd fight over who got to fuck me first."

We regarded him hopefully.

"Sorry, I'm here to devour souls."

"Can't you do both?"

***

Liddy again eyed the pigskin case. He smiled, then looked back at me. "So."

"So."

"Are you here to do bad things to me?"

"I'm here to right the spiritual order of this house."

"Which means—"

"I'm here to send you to Hell."

***

I didn't want the demon to devour my soul. I paged nervously through the grimoire. Liddy looked on.

"You can't do anything. You're trapped in the circle. We used kosher salt."

The demon smiled, touched the salt, and put some on his tongue. He then stepped out of the circle with ease.

"You made a boo-boo," he said while pointing a thumb over his shoulder. "That only works on virgin flesh." And, proving that even the homeliest and least socially adroit among you have a chance at love, the dweebster you scavenged was not."

The basement door opened above us. Light flooded in. Susan, Liddy's mom, peered down. "Liddell? What's going on down there? Why do I smell smoke?"

The demon beamed. "Hey, Mom!"

She came down the stairs. "Who the hell are you?"

Liddy and I froze.

"Your Reverend Perry was right to decry the free library's occult collection. Your son and his friend used it to conjure me."

Her expression was no bullshit. "Are you here to sell them drugs? Is that what this is, Liddell? I'm gonna call the cops."

The demon smiled and pointed a finger at her. She exploded, splattering the basement. A fine mist lingered. Her remains covered us.

It smiled at Liddy. "Don't lie. Part of you wanted that to happen."

"Mom? Liddy?" It was Liddy's little sister. Just nine. She stirred Liddy from his horror. "Jilly! Get out! N—"

Suddenly the demon was gone. Liddy smiled wickedly. He turned towards the stairs. "Jilly. It's okay. C'mere. We've got a surprise for you."

She poked her head towards us. "Really?!"

"Jilly, no—"

Liddy smiled at me. Then he vaporized Jilly. When her blood splashed his face he blinked, then regarded me with horror.

"Run!"

I hesitated.

"Now!"

I ran.

***

I returned in time to see paramedics rolling the first body out. Another paramedic vomited on the lawn. I slipped into the house before anyone could stop me. There, in the parlour, hung Liddy, neck broken, with a deviant smile.

***

"The demon left me behind to haunt this place, which I couldn't really do because nobody wanted to live in the murder house. Until these idiots showed up, at least. You know, I did you solid. I could have just splattered you. Or left you to take the rap. Right now, you'd be funny farmed, eating clozapine porridge, and dreading the allegedly female charge nurse's surreptitious affections. Maybe that would be better, considering what you've become."

"I serve God and his people."

Liddy laughed. "Spare me. Do you know what Hell is like? I mean, besides the fact that the only music they play there is The Carpenters? Hell is all the world's most interesting people, doomed for displeasing your preening fascist of a boss. And you're his muscle."

I bowed my head and prayed silently. Then I rose.

Liddy looked nervous. "So, this is it? Hi, great to catch up, '[e]xorcizo te'? You know, you could have been me!"

I opened the bag and withdrew a purple stole, kissed it, and put it around the back of my neck. I then extracted and arrayed on the coffee table between us two bottles of holy water, a cruet, paten, and rite book.

"Oh, this is exquisitely depraved, even for your Roman church! I was your best friend! I haven't seen you in twenty years, and you're playing exterminator!"

I opened the rite book.

"I was thirteen! It was your idea!"

I took a deep breath, then splashed him with holy water from the extra bottle I kept in my jacket pocket. He screamed.

***

Mom stormed in upon hearing the scream. Even though I told her not to. Even though the walls had bled. And she even brought Billy and Hannah.

"What's going on? We heard a—Kendall? Why are you here?"

When I'd last seen him, Liddy was wiry and roughly handsome. But that body died twenty years ago. Now, thanks to her fortuitous timing, he was Kendall, a gorgeous, nineteen-year-old brunette in tight jeans who was supposed to be studying the sociology of displaced peoples at community college downtown.

Mom flashed shock. "Is it gone?"

I verged on tears.

"What's going on?"

I looked at Liddy, now Kendall. He smiled. Then he pointed his finger at Billy, toying obliviously with Mom's phone. His pulverized remains cushioned the blow when the phone, formerly in his grasp, hit the floor. Mom came next, then Hannah. I shielded myself from the gore with a throw I found on an adjacent couch. I threw it over the remains once Liddy finished.

I then gathered the exorcism kit back into the pigskin bag.

"You're keeping that?"

He was right. Everything was gooey. I chucked it all in the fireplace.

Liddy smiled lasciviously. "I knew the old Jonesy was lurking somewhere in there."

He leaned towards me while pointing his thumbs towards his shoulders. "Maybe someday I'll let you hit this."

I smiled. I mean, he was my best friend. And I did owe him. I try not to think about it too much. Thinking about things too much, trying to fix what I can't control, made me a bag man for a preening fascist.

This time, at least, we picked the right meat.

ME, AGAIN

I was twenty-nine and felt seventy-nine. And none of this would have been necessary if I were nineteen. They staggered the pain meds to avoid making me a junkie. An all-liquid diet to heal wounds and protect stitches. I never thought I'd tire of cucumber water, but I have. By now, the wounds had healed, and my face looked itself again. Not nineteen, more like twenty-five, but still terrific. Now I was indulging three days of skin treatments to ensure that any whisper of a scar would fade. I once did one of those genetic ancestry tests out of sheer vanity and discovered I was mostly Scottish, but also Italian and Chinese. The Italian genes were good. My skin didn't age horribly. Still, twenty-nine is twenty-nine, even with my genes.

Mortality is harder when you're beautiful.

***

Discretion is the better part of vanity, especially in a place where the beautiful come to get ugly. So, for $10,000 a day, the clinic ensured total discretion. No mobile phones. No cameras. And, aside from dedicated cables for business purposes, no internet. Mirrors were prescription-only. And the staff were trained to be flat-faced, be it beauty or beast before them. Two entrance/exits, one of which required a helicopter. All clients were identified by number.

Several of the doctors were headquartered in Beverly Hills and had reality TV shows. They signed onerous nondisclosures to work here. And the last paparazzo who showed up was politely turned away after being assured that every bad thing he'd ever done would be publicized if he returned.

***

So, safe and bored, I watched television, or the male nurses obviously chosen for looks as much as talent.

"Number eleven."

I looked up. It was Miguel, my favourite nurse, here for my rubdown.

"Miguel. Is it time to grope me?"

He smiled. "We prefer to call it 'therapeutic massage,' ma'am."

"Of course."

Lucky him. My body was one of the most desirable on Earth. Even at twenty-nine. Even after a mild cosmetic touch-up. A billionaire once offered me a hundred thousand dollars to see my breasts. A million if he could touch them.

Which is why I was shocked to see them on television, for free. Suddenly, I wasn't in the clinic. I was on a yacht in the Mediterranean, topless. "What the shit?!"

Miguel looked up. "What?"

"On television. It's me."

The show was a flashy gossipfest. The anchor paired big tits and a plunging neckline with a breathless delivery. "Is that Greer MacLaren doing the topless mega yacht thing? Sure looks like it. Wonder who's swabbing *her* deck?"

"Those look like your tits, chica."

"Yeah, they sure do." I smiled at him. "Not that you're supposed notice that kind of thing."

Europeans eschewed American nudity hang-ups, so we got a great look. Drone with a telephoto video lens. Then somebody onboard blasted the drone with a shotgun, ending the feed. The woman looked like me. Strike that. The woman was me. Except younger and prettier.

"You got a twin?"

"Not that I know of."

Miguel raised his hands eagerly.

"Therapeutic massage, Miguel. Therapeutic massage."

***

I didn't think too much about it during the balance of my recuperation. And then, the day before I was to be discharged, I turned up dead.

Same gossipfest twentysomething hottie, tits on parade. She looked genuinely upset but still couldn't wait to tell the story. "We're receiving unconfirmed reports that supermodel Greer MacLaren has been found dead on a beach in the Seychelles. We have amateur video of what is purported to be her remains. This is extremely disturbing, and we recommend that—Oh my God!"

She barfed. Right on air. All over her tits. To be fair, the beach scene was pretty gnarly. The body was relatively fresh. It was definitely me. Or, half of me. My wrists were slashed the right way, vertical not horizontal. Not that that mattered. I was gone below the waist, intestines trailing, Cthulhu-like, from my belly. Then some crab-like sea creatures flooded out, back into the surf. That's when she hurled.

Miguel was rubbing me, and it was sublime.

"Miguel, my legs are still there, right?"

"Yup."

"And they're still magnificent, right?"

"They are. So is your ass. Not that I'm supposed to notice that kind of thing."

I chuckled. "Thanks."

An orderly appeared with an encrypted satellite phone. "It's your agent."

I took the phone. "Martine?"

She was hysterical. "Oh, thank God you're alive!"

"Of course I'm alive."

"Then who's that in the Seychelles?"

"I don't know. But I'm going to find out."

***

I didn't get a chance. The Victoria medical examiner's office burned the remains before the police could investigate. They said it was a mix-up. The good news was that my would-be near death experience popped my Q and doubled my Instagram and other social media hits. I'd like to think people were grateful that their favourite piece of ass was intact.

I tried to shrug the weirdness off. Someone who looked a lot like me. It happens. Maybe I'm a little less special than I thought. Or a little more, now that my doppelgänger's dead. I took an alprazolam to ward off the creeps.

***

I was dozing when I showed up again. The gate guard was puzzled how I got out without him noticing. I explained that I'd helicoptered out for a private lunch in Zurich and opted to return by car. Turns out Hans (that was his name) was a fan.

"Selfie?" God knows what kind of weird picture collection of me he had on his phone.

"Of course!"

He took five, then let me pass, wishing me a good day.

Heidi, the receptionist, was also a big fan. The staff were accustomed to famous faces and instructed not to fawn. Still, Heidi, only twenty-two and irrepressibly enthusiastic, couldn't help herself.

"Ms. MacLaren! I didn't know you'd left."

I smiled at her. "I didn't."

BANG! I shot her throat with a .45 auto pistol. BANG! Down went the security guard studying his phone in an adjacent kiosk.

People ran. To no avail. There were two exits, and the one I wasn't blocking required a helicopter. BANG! Orderly. BANG! Nurse. BANG! Plastic-surgery-addicted septuagenarian. BANG! BANG! Two cleft palate charity cases flown in from Albania.

I rose from my bed, terrified. Miguel scrambled into my room, shut the door, and braced himself against it. The shots came closer. The screams were fewer. Then I heard a helicopter approaching the roof.

BANG! BANG! BANG! Three shots through my door. And Miguel. Crimson spotted his white uniform. He fell forward. The door opened. And there I was. In a smart, black ensemble with a turtleneck sweater and cargo pants. Hot. I pointed the gun at myself.

Then I holstered the pistol, drew another, longer pistol, and fired. It was a tranquilizer gun. I subsided as I approached the bed.

***

Gossipfest was on. Same hottie anchor. Same revealing clothes. Same enthusiasm to tell a horrible story. "Ohmygod it's like a total splatterama at Pic Élevé, a hyper-exclusive clinic in Switzerland long rumoured to serve convalescing billionaires and celebrities. We obtained this exclusive camera phone footage of the victims. Authorities have yet to name any suspects or even speculate what motivated the killings."

There it was: Towering windows allowing perfect mountain views. Marble accents with stainless steel lighting fixtures. Fresh flowers in leaded glass vases on brushed steel tables. And staff and patients, dead on the floor, blood congealed around them.

"There are unconfirmed reports that supermodel Greer MacLaren was at Pic Élevé recuperating from an undisclosed medical procedure. However, this is an unconfirmed report, so don't build your teddy bear shrines just yet."

"I'm building mine."

I looked up. There I was. And again. And again. Three of me, all about eighteen, all perfect. I wore only bikinis.

"Where am I?"

Another voice. "You're home, darling."

I knew him. I couldn't recall the name. I'd met him at some party and he offered me ten thousand dollars to eat mangos out of my ass. I politely declined.

"You're—"

"Miles Pravesh—"

"Mr. Mango."

"Ha. Yes. Well, that wasn't one of my finer moments. I was overwhelmed with champagne, and then with you, and well, my baser instincts took hold."

"Of course they did."

"Well, you are you."

I gestured at my doppelgängers. "And so are they?"

They looked at him. He nodded. They looked at me, then spoke in unison: "We are."

The middle one scrutinized me. "She's old."

"You're direct."

I looked back at Miles. "So, I have a million questions, but I guess 'What the fuck is going on here?' pretty well sums them up."

He smiled, then extended his hand. I took it.

***

"It all started with D-Enable."

D-Enable was the genetic testing service I'd used. They were supposed to be discreet.

"Ten million dollars for your genetic code."

Miles gestured towards a magnificent machine, a brushed steel box with plexiglass on four sides. Within, via relentless robotic arms, another me materialized: bones, muscles, vessels, nerves.

"And a hundred million for this. The South Korean government stopped its inventor from finalizing it. So, he came to me. International waters area a bad place for human rights. Anyway, after a bunch of false starts…"

He pointed again at the doppelgängers. "Success."

"What about the Mini-Me that washed up in Victoria?"

"Alas, ten percent of you go mental and suicide. It cost me fifty K to disappear the others."

The cloning process was almost complete. The arms dressed sleek muscles in flawless skin.

I heard muted moans coming from the next room. I pointed towards the clamour. "Is that what I think it is?"

"It is. Do you want to see? It's really quite something. A fleshy metaphor of our self-adoring postmodernity."

He keyed his phone, and two sliding doors parted. Before us was me, times ten, aged arguably legal to twenty-five, in a furious orgy.

Miles put an arm around my shoulders. "After the mid-twenties, they lose their savour."

A chill hit me.

He smiled. "Don't worry. They're so stoned they don't feel a thing."

I forced a smile. "So why am I here? I mean, I'm twenty-nine, and I just went under the knife. I mean, I'm practically nostalgia."

"Because I suspect that the original, dings and all, still beats the knock-offs." He studied my face. "Excellent work. Really, really superb."

"Wow, I'm so glad you approve. And I can't wait for you to burn me alive."

I looked at the others. "That's what he's going to do. He's going to kill you. Don't you care?!"

In unison: "We are honoured to die for him."

He pulled me closer. "We tweaked the genetic code to make them submissive. You know, like the clones in *Star Wars*. You can't all be Boba Fett."

The cloning chamber beeped. The clone emerged from it, flawless, slick with what I guess was some kind of nutrient solution. She approached me, then touched my cheek.

Tears streamed from her eyes. "I'm sorry."

"What?"

She seized a leaded crystal vase from a nearby stable, spilling the flowers within to the floor. She smashed it, then ruptured her perfect belly with the jagged base.

The other clones backed away, horrified.

Miles seemed unmoved. "Like I said, ten percent self-destruct. It's a kink."

His grip loosened, and I dropped. I grabbed a vase shard and rose.

Miles panicked and looked at the unholy trinity. "Help me!"

They stared soundlessly at their fallen sister, all but bled out on the floor, shuddering in her afterbirth.

I've dated a lot of masters of the universe. They're usually soft. Miles was, too. I slashed his throat and kept slashing until I hit bone. His blood mingled with the clone's as they died together on the floor.

I dropped the shard, then to my knees, and vomited. Then I wept.

***

It's been three months since I escaped. And the clone problem has only gotten worse. Miles' death triggered a perverse gesture of magnanimity: My genetic code went online, free for anyone to download. And, while there are only a few 3-D genetic printers on the planet capable of fabricating me, I started turning up at polo matches, casinos, and movie premiers with rich weirdoes. I suppose I commodified myself long before this happened, but at least then I controlled it. Now the best I can hope for is a reality show where I live with my other selves in contrived romantic and comic situations. And hopefully there won't be too many of those.

Immortality is harder when you're beautiful.

GERTIE

Goethe "Gertie" Rommler murdered twenty-seven women during his well-publicized reign of terror. He fancied himself a scourge of feminism and other progressive mindsets despoiling women's beauty and mystery as seducers and helpmeets of men. Antifeminists embracing his crusade against inauthentic femininity dubbed him the "Bitch Ripper." He was America's greatest misogynist.

Gertie is thought to have died in a fire at the mental hospital where he'd been confined after being found mentally unfit to stand trial. The explosion, caused by a gas leak owing to deferred maintenance, obliterated many of the residents outright. They were buried in empty graves.

Prior to his hospitalization, Gertie lived in a neo-gothic manse looming incongruously in a formerly prosperous Indianapolis city and built by an occultist who got rich selling wealthy widows bogus communions with dead relatives. Kraft Rommler, Gertie's enterprising nephew and sole heir, cared neither for the occult or his uncle. He did, however, recognize a good business opportunity and therefore turned the place into the Goethe Rommler Museum of Murder, ostensibly not to profit from the suffering of Gertie's victims, but, rather, "to remember with due gravity and circumspection a dark time in American cultural history."

The museum included a gift stop, which sold Gertie's certified possessions (at least, certified to have been found in a storage locker a fan bought rights to after Gertie stopped paying the rent). They included underbleached underpants and family vacation videos depicting Gertie's penchant for burning things. The cashier, an underemployed satanic priestess, would curse your purchases for an extra ten bucks.

It was opening day. More than a hundred people showed, not bad for Shitty, Indiana. Black balloon bunches adorned the gargoyles flanking the main entrance. A few reporters lingered outside, outnumbered by heavyset protesters pleading the victims' human dignity.

Two patrons were particularly compelling: Jenny Sales, a coed writing a Semiotics of Violence term paper, and Melissa Irving, a journalist writing for a feminist webzine whose editors probably advocated chemically castrating every heterosexual male on earth. Jenny was centre-of-gravity beautiful; perpetual frowning shadowed Melissa's otherwise undeniable appeal. Both had requested opening day access for the projects. I cheerfully obliged.

I introduced myself. "Hey, people. I'm your tour guide. Would anyone like a gastrointestinal distress bag before we begin?"

I brandished some. Smiles, except for Melissa. "Hi. I'm Melissa Irving. I'm reviewing this little…"

"Homicide hutch? Murder manse? Artisanal abattoir?"

Her frown increased. "I'm reviewing it for *Wave4.com*. It's a feminist web magazine. Can I ask a question up front?"

"Sure."

"Goethe Rommler murdered twenty-four women and defiled their remains. And you're monetizing that. How do you justify all this?"

"Twenty-seven."

"What?"

"He murdered twenty-seven women. As to your question, we hope preserving depravity's fruits for public inspection will keep future generations from bearing them."

That wasn't the answer she expected. I think she was pissed that she had already to re-write her column.

We came to a black velvet curtain separating the exhibits from unpaying eyes. "Before we commence, I'd like to play a short recording Gertie made just before his hospitalization. It's quite famous, and I'm sure you've all heard it before. Still, it offers context to what you're about to see."

I pushed a button on a remote control in my pocket.

Gertie's voice boomed over concealed speakers. "I think of my work as a quest for love. All my life, I've searched for the right woman to love me. And I have yet to find her. Instead, I've found countless disappointments. And I've let my disappointment get the better of me. But I have faith that I will find her. I know that, when she sees all that I've done, she'll understand. St. Paul was right. Life without love isn't really life. Life without love is a husk, movement without action, touch without sensation, breath without blood."

I turned to the group, a little teary-eyed. Jenny smiled. Melissa smirked. The others were delighted, or repelled and delighted.

"I wouldn't be surprised if the girl of Gertie's dreams is among you today. I mean, it is opening day."

I turned to the curtain. "Last chance. There's life on this side of the curtain, and life after you've seen what's on the other side. They're quite different."

Everyone remained.

"Oh, good." I pulled the curtain and guided them inside.

***

Within was a series of installations commemorating Gertie's greatest hits, each titled with the date and location of the crime. The first display featured a colourful hotdog cart, umbrella extended. Flanking it were portraits of the victims.

"'April 7, 2014, Chicago, Illinois.' We chose understated titles for overstated crimes. However, Gertie referred to it as—"

"Hot Doggerel!" Jenny pressed against the crimson velvet rope designed to keep fans from consummating their various fantasies.

"This is one of Gertie's best capers. It started when he took two women on a tour of old

Chicago, culminating with a visit to an abandoned slaughterhouse. His dates, Irma Myers and Maxine Todd, were liberal-minded MFA poetry students looking to disrupt prosperity's doldrums. He dogged them. Then he hot dogged them. And then he fed them to roughly three hundred people."

Jenny pointed at the City of Chicago's official lab test results of the meat, a large reproduction of which was framed beside the cart. "Long pig, double mustard!"

Melissa blanched, then smirked. "You're exaggerating. There's no way you could get three hundred hot dogs out of two people."

"Sure, he could. The MFAs were triple-XL. There were leftovers. But I'm getting ahead of myself."

I turned to Melissa. "You could say that turning women into meat sandwiches symbolizes the patriarchy's subjection of women to its demands. I mean, Gertie's practically a prophet, right?"

She smirked, and I couldn't tell if she was amused or plotting my death. Maybe both.

I regarded the rest of the group. "I'm not sure what the gift shop hot dogs contain; alas, I'm fairly certain it's conventional fare."

***

Next came "June 3, 2014, Poland, Indiana." It featured a mock-up of Gamma Omicron Rho sorority house at the local college. "Gertie called this misfortune—"

Jenny's enthusiasm waxed again. "GOR Whores!"

The butcher knives Gertie used stood, still bloodied, in a transparent case beside the front porch. Portraits of the departed sisters, along with crime scene photos identifying their remains, hung above them.

Melissa approached one of the knife cases. "Are the knives supposed to correspond to the victims?"

"That's the idea. We used the coroner's report to guestimate. I doubt even Gertie would remember those details. Anyway, for the unenlightened among you (though I doubt there are any), June 3, 2014 is when Gertie Bundied a bunch of sorority sisters after a super glue bender. Some people say those Stacy bitches had it coming. Not me, of course. College coeds are the light shining us forward into a better world. Anyway, I know Bundy did it first. But that doesn't mean it didn't need to happen again. There's something sublime about murdering coed hotties in the prime of life, especially when they're engaged in secret initiation rituals incorporating lesbian grooming. Better to die beautiful and tragic than to wither away as some harpy corporate lawyer managing male gaze complaints."

Jenny again pressed against the velvet rope.

I smiled at her. "Well?"

"I mean, props for the set-up. But, didn't you get the film?"

"Ah, yes. The film."

Melissa blanched. "You wouldn't—"

"We would, actually. But we can't show it. Litigation. Some of the victims' parents, well, you understand…"

Jenny snarled. "Actually, I don't. I mean, it's a public record now."

"Actually, it's not. Gertie' estate owns the rights to it, and therefore this museum controls it."

She regarded me hopefully. "I've heard there are bootleg copies and people play drinking games with them."

"Alas, contempt of court's a bitch. So, sorry, can't do it." I smiled. "Not that we won't once the litigation is resolved. Like, instantly."

***

The final installation was "May 1, 2014, San Francisco, California." The set featured a blandly professional medical clinic waiting room, a series of beiges and pastels complete with middle- and low-brow magazines. Smooth jazz played from ceiling speakers. An espresso bar adorned one wall, a massage area the other. Incongruously, the wall was covered with portraits of stylized hand grenades and other hangings draped in black. There was a door slightly ajar adjacent the receptionist's desk. Above it, painted in cursive script: "Never apologize for wanting to be free."

Jenny was against the rope. "Smooth Jazz Abortion Clinic."

I smiled. "Right. That's what he called it. Extraordinarily poor taste, even for me. Still, probably Gertie's greatest work."

I walked to the door and pushed it open. Automatic lights illuminated a gynaecologist's office, complete with lurid diagrams and sparkling instruments. "Gertie despised abortion. He said that it represented a woman's fundamental betrayal of her life's purpose. So, one day, he subdued the clinic's owner, donned some scrubs, and gave it the old college try."

I pushed a button and the black coverings fell away. Beneath were crime scene photos of the patients, all of whom died of internal bleeding while waiting for their post-scrape lattes.

The tour group was silent, circumspect. This crime was perhaps the purest manifestation of Gertie's hatred of women. I eyed them. "Well?"

Jenny smiled. "Can I sit in the abortion chair?"

***

Another black curtain separated the tour from the gift shop. I paused before withdrawing it.

"On the other side of this curtain is the gift shop. I'm sure that you'll all find a treasured keepsake to memorialize today's adventure. Most of Gertie's pornography collection remains in stock. I assure you it's legal in most jurisdictions. Plus, we have all the hate mail he got in hospital. He read every letter.

And, don't forget, our cashier Barbara will curse your purchases for a small surcharge."

Melissa smiled. "I thought Gertie was an atheist. In fact, it's one of the few things I admire about him."

"There's more than one?"

She looked embarrassed.

"You're correct. Still, I like to think he appreciates the extra touch, woo or no woo. Anyway, thanks for indulging us our little labour of love. Please come back. And remember that Saturdays are family discount days."

As the patrons departed, I turned to Jenny and Melissa. "Jenny? Melissa? Could you hang back for a moment?"

They did, along with one overeager goth guy wearing more makeup than they did. "Is there some kind of Easter egg?"

I frowned. "Yes. In the gift shop."

"No, I mean-"

"Sorry. Invitation only."

He departed, miffed.

Jenny flashed sceptical. "So why are we trailing?"

Melissa smiled at me. "Is this the clothing optional part of the tour?"

I laughed. They smiled uneasily.

"Do you want to see the real museum?"

"What?"

"What you saw is for the hoi polloi and grandma's birthday adventure. It's a joke. The real tour's in the basement. We found some deeply evil shit down there."

They looked at each other, then me. Then, together: "Why us?"

"Because I think you respect him. Not the same way, but with the same vigour. And that's what he always wanted."

They didn't say no.

***

Imagine Gacy doing a Vatican catacomby thing.

Three MILF joggers, late thirties, trendily spandexed and entombed behind plexiglass, putrefaction smears partly obscuring the view.

Jenny pressed her nose against the glass.

Melissa was more composed. "You didn't tell—"

"The police? No. They'd shut us down. And we'd probably get demolished. Or firebombed. I mean, look what happened to Gacy's house. And Gein's. So much history, lost to madness. It's like they burned the Library at Alexandria. Twice."

Melissa turned to me and smiled. "Speaking of burning, how did you escape?"

Jenny looked at her. "What are you talking about?"

Melissa continued. "The hospital fire. He didn't die." She looked at my face, then stroked my jawline.

Jenny recognized me at last. "Gertie?"

Melissa nodded. "You're much more handsome in person. Even post-plastic. I mean, my parents were freaked when I put your pictures on my wall and luckily the shrink they hired said my fixation was normal for adolescent hormones. And it didn't occur to me till after the tour. This whole thing. Your whole body of work. You're looking for the right girl. This whole museum. . . it's your interview process."

I teared up. "'For now we see through a glass, darkly...'"

Melissa smiled. "'[B]ut then face to face...'"

I continued. "'Now I know in part...'"

She concluded. "'But then shall I know even as I am known.' St. Paul was right. Life without love is a husk. You knew. You knew you'd find me."

"I hoped."

We embraced, then kissed. Then we turned to Jenny.

"Jenny, dear, would you like to go behind the rope?"

"What?"

I handed Melissa a straight razor. She smiled and flicked it open. "Ready, Jenny?"

"I am."

The pain was sudden, sharp. I was light-headed. I looked down to see blood rushing to the floor, soaking my pants. Then I was on the floor.

"I can't believe you kissed him."

Melissa sighed. "I can."

She smiled at me. "I wasn't lying. Part of me really likes him." She hesitated.

"But?"

"But the better part of me just wants to watch him die."

I smiled as I faded out.

I had found her, and she me.

THE SLICE OF LIFE

Morrissey Memorial High School is for ass kickers. The smart kids, one percenter progeny destined to stay one percent. Half go Ivy. We're all relentless. And we're all super nice. Especially when we're stepping on each other. Blame the Addy.

I was streamlining the local food bank's distribution network (colleges love that shit) when it suddenly all became too much. Or, should I say, not enough. I mean, I was feeding the hungry, even if giving them meat abraded my vegan sensibilities. I should have been jazzed. Instead, it was just another application box to check.

So, I started cutting myself. Not a lot. Just enough to take the edge off my self-loathing. Cutting releases endorphins, which distract me from myself. So, there I was, sitting in a gender-neutral bathroom stall like some kind of junkie. It was just a pen knife, but they'd still suspend me, and I wouldn't even get into community college. I hid it in a loose wall tile a few inches from the floor. School always felt like prison anyway.

"Hey Jill Pill. I know you're in there. If you're holding, I'll snitch you. That is—"

I opened the stall door. My friend Maureen stood there, smiling. "Unless you share."

"If only."

"What are you doing?"

I hesitated.

"Don't worry. We're alone."

She drew closer. "Oh my God, you're bleeding!"

"Just a little."

"You're cutting yourself."

"Yup. And no, I don't need an intervention."

Maureen smiled knowingly. Then she hiked her skirt to expose her inner thigh.

"Mo's going 'mo?"

Then I saw them. One to two inches each, crisscrossing scars.

"What?"

"Yeah, dumbass, welcome to the club. We call it the 'slice of life.'"

"We?"

"Yeah. Me, and Liz, and some other people. Sometimes we cut each other."

"That sounds hot."

"It's not like that. I mean, I think Liz wants it to be like that, but really, it isn't."

She looked at my knife. "I hope you disinfected that. I mean, you could get an infection."

I looked at the knife. She was right. I used only a kerchief to clean it.

"Ya gotta bleach it to be sure. You don't want opportunistic infections. Do you know how much evil shit lives on your skin?"

Panic flooded me. "Thanks. Now I need to cut myself again."

"We meet at the old grammar school. The one they've been planning to tear down but never do. In the boiler room. You know, like Freddy Krueger, pre-cooked."

She held out her hand.
I took it.

***

Dolores Wurther's sophomore honours English class was the only non-deadening subject in my college trudge. I know, who does sophomore honours classes? We do.

Ms. Wurther took some pain away. She asked big questions, consequences be damned. She didn't reinforce people in their conceits, like most of the other teachers, who dwelled in constant fear of being adjudged insensitive. She got what it was like to be no longer a kid but not quite an adult. Her classes were hopelessly oversubscribed. She taught extra periods to accommodate everyone; Roughly a third of us had studied under her.

"So, people, since we're reading about existentialism, does anyone want to explain what we're doing here?"

"English literature helps us understand the oppressive structures embedded in our culture, thereby making it easier for us to deconstruct and overthrow them."

Groans erupted. Liz, the overachiever's overachiever, was again trying too hard.

I spoke up. "Because we have to."

Ms. Wurther smiled. "Continue."

"So we can go to the right college, so we can go to the right grad school, so we can work for the right corporation until it fires us because we're too old and expensive and dying of cancer."

Everybody laughed. Except for Liz.

Ms. Wurther smiled. "That's a bit dark."

Liz smiled.

"But I think it's mostly right."

Liz frowned.

"I mean, how many of you burn to read Shakespeare and Dickens?"

Liz's hand went up.

"We know, Liz, we know."

She withdrew it sheepishly.

"I mean, yeah, these guys—you're right about that Liz, mostly guys—even George Eliot had to publish as a dude—they aren't utterly irrelevant to our lives. They got the human condition, and the human condition is a constant across time. But how are they going to help you process data in a cubicle while freaking about the co-worker who's gonna snitch you to HR for some bullshit offense against their sensibilities? And all this while the C-suiters are plotting to automate your job?"

The bell rang.

"Think about it, people."

***

After field hockey practice, and reading to the blind, and feeding the homeless (Mondays were a bitch), I encountered Liz. She pulled up beside me in her convertible. We weren't friends, but we didn't hate each other. "Hey."

"Hey."

She held up a smoothie. "Mo said you'd be hungry."

I took it. "Strawberry banana. How did you know?"

"Duh, who doesn't like strawberry banana?"

"Good point."

She smiled. "Mo said you'd come."

"Come where?"

"To our little safe space."

I looked at my watch.

"Don't worry. You'll have plenty of time to do your homework. And if anyone knows about having enough time to do your homework, it's me."

I hesitated.

"C'mon. It's like safe sex, but with edged weapons."

I acquiesced.

***

The place felt like an abandoned chapel, a gothic husk. Liz led me through the front doors. The chains keeping them closed slacked enough to admit the sufficiently slender. We hit the staircase just to the left, then the basement, then the boiler room.

Inside were Mo and most of the rest of the honours English class. Some juniors and seniors were also there. The others viewed me suspiciously, as if their exclusive club was suddenly less exclusive.

Black candles illuminated everything.

"The candles are a nice touch. Nice and Satan-y."

Ms. Wurther smiled. "Jill! We're so glad you're here."

"Ms. Wurther?"

"Yeah, I know. I'm pretty sure that superintending the cutting club is a felony, so don't blab."

She turned to the others. "Who wants to start?"

"Me!" Liz again, trying too hard.

Ms. Wurther frowned. "Liz, you've gotta heal, baby."

"No. I'm ready."

She doffed her Oxford button-down. Dozens of scars defaced her abdomen.

Before Ms. Wurther could object, Liz palmed a switchblade, popped it, and drew it skilfully through the scar tissue. Blood blossomed.

"Jesus Christ!" I put my hand to my mouth.

Ms. Wurther regarded the rest of us with a nervous smile. "Who else wants to go? How about you, Jill?"

She tossed me a small package. I opened its sealed paper. Inside was a fresh razor blade.

"Gotta keep things clean. The last thing Morrissey Memorial High School needs is a hepatitis outbreak."

I froze up. Liz was at my side in an instant. "I'll do it!"

"Manners, gunner, manners."

Mo approached me. "I gotcha, girl." She put an arm around me while deftly freeing the razor from its packaging. "Ready?"

"I guess. I mean, I haven't even—"

It was a clean slash across my shoulder. First nothing, then brilliant pain. I staggered. Mo eased me to the floor.

Liz was indignant. "That's what I want! Why can't I have that?"

Mo smirked. "I don't think she swings that way, hon."

Liz flipped her off.

Ms. Wurther rose. "Calm down, people."

Liz teared up. "I'm serious. It's like I can't feel anymore. Anything. It's this goddamned school. And then four more years of goddamned school."

I was still outside myself.

Ms. Wurther went to Liz. "Liz, it's okay."

"No, it's not!"

She embraced Liz. Then Liz kissed her. She indulged Liz for a moment, then gently pushed her away. Liz bolted.

I was finally coming back. Mo held a cloth to my arm. "It's got antibiotic ointment on it. Scarring should be minimal. I mean, unless you like the scars."

Ms. Wurther smiled. "Maybe we should pack it in tonight, people."

***

It started the next day.

We were in the auditorium for all-school assembly. There was a pep rally. Mo and I were cheerleaders because the boys were still dumb no matter how smart they were on paper. Liz was out sick.

Just before our routine ended, everybody looked above us in terror.

We looked up. Liz stood on the drama club's lighting rigging. She wore her cheerleader outfit and clutched her pom-poms. A noose encircled her neck.

"Hey everybody. I just wanted to let you know that you won't have to worry about competing with me to get into college. Or anything else, actually. I'm getting out. It's the only moral response to—to—all of this. All of you. Peace out."

She jumped. Her neck snapped. She shuddered in the air, then was still.

All I remember after that are screams.

***

They bused in grief counsellors and suicide preventers from the local liberal arts college who grooved on world saving. We re-assembled so everybody could talk about how they felt.

Rodge Porter, angling to be Jesus, stood up. "I'd like to say something."

Jesus God please no.

"I'm personally devastated by Elizabeth's passing. I think that we lose a sense of our humanity sometimes in our vigorous pursuit of excellence. We need to accept that it's okay to feel. To reach out—"

"OHMYGOD! NOOOOOO! NOOOOOOOO!"

***

The faculty wouldn't let us see. But the video went live right after the bodies were discovered. A senior, a junior, and a freshman had suicided in the bathroom near the auditorium. Sally, Idina, and Barb. They were all on the field hockey team. Sally was being recruited by all the Ivies. Idina and Barb were on the same path. And now they were gone, each propped up against a toilet in one of the stalls, bleeding efficiently into the drain.

Sally was their leader. She narrated the video. "Jill was right. Why do we work so hard and make so many sacrifices, just so we can work hard and make sacrifices, and work hard and make sacrifices? What, so I can drive big and shop big? We're done. We're just done."

Sally slashed her wrists vertically, each arm methodically, then handed to razor to Idina, who, after following suit, handed it to Barb.

The principal tried and failed to corral us. We crowded the hall, flooding out of the auditorium, quiet, mournful. Then our phones buzzed again.

Another video, another bathroom, another suicide trio. This time, Myra, Trini, and Bill. Trini was their leader. "We're following Sally. Which is funny, because we're sick of following. Maybe our witness will give pause to everybody who submitted us to this—this—insane machine we've been fed into and that our kids will be fed into."

There was a muted voice behind him. He turned to it. "What?"

Then he turned back. "Oh, you're right. I guess we're not having kids."

He brandished a scalpel. "My dad said this is the sharpest knife in the world. Let's see if he's right."

He disembowelled himself. And, after a brief disagreement about who would go next, Myra and Bill did, too.

The faculty freaked. They forced us into the auditorium, using the school's security resource officer as muscle. Most of us were too stunned to resist. The principal, former military, took control. She turned to the dean of students.

"Call 911. Then sweep the rest of the bathrooms. After that we need to—"

Our phones interrupted her.

Gasps flooded the room.

More videos, these individual. Different kids slashing themselves: wrists, throats, bellies, femoral arteries.

The principal shouted. "Everyone! Eyes front!"

"Teachers! Doors!" Faculty blocked the doors.

"John, do a headcount. Omar, collect everybody's phones."

John was the faculty dean. Omar was the athletic director.

We were too stunned to protest. I sat next to Mo. "What the fuck?"

She was excited. "Maybe it's a cluster!"

"A cluster?"

"A suicide cluster! It happens when kids copycat suicide each other. I read about it happening at some high school in Minnesota."

"I think I'd commit suicide if I had to live in Minnesota, too."

Mo smiled.

The principal continued. "Okay people, we're gonna do a wellness check. We need everybody to stand up, row by row, starting in the back, just to make sure everybody's okay."

The third row in, five people didn't stand. More screams.

The principal and other faculty swarmed. The kids were dead. Somehow, they'd managed surreptitiously to cut themselves. Femoral arteries: They'd bled out onto floor. Blood rivulets just now reached my feet.

"What the hell is going on?"

The principal at last went gestapo. "Strip search! All students!"

"NO!" Ms. Wurther stood up. "Are you insane?!"

The principal was pissed. "Dolores, sit down! You have no authority here!"

"You're right, I don't. And that's the problem, isn't it?"

She went to the stage. "I know why this is happening. You don't see it, but I do. They're tired of it. The micromanaging. The dehumanizing fetishization of success. Success at all costs. It was the same when I went here. And when I went to 'the right college.' It was the same kids following their parents' dreams following their parents' dreams. And that's why I returned. To disrupt that. And I'm just getting started."

She held up a straight razor. "Now, people!"

Half the remaining students brandished razorblades. Then everybody started cutting. Blood rioted into the air.

I looked at Mo. She was poised to slash her throat.

I grabbed her hand. "Mo, don't."

She smiled. "She's right." She handed me her razor. "Come with me."

I took it. She nodded tenderly.

The cut was sublime. Mo put my head in her lap. As I faded away, I saw Mo's throat come open.

At last, the madness subsided.

#meatoo

Necrophilia is a felony in California. It wasn't always, but it is now. Of course, for my clients, that probably makes it more fun.

I'm Anton Mack, undertaker to the stars. But not how you think. The only things celebrities care about after they're dead are concealing the real cause of death (usually drugs, sometimes a social disease) and/or dick size (cell phones make that harder to enforce; though, if you slip me a G, I can remove and incinerate it). The payoffs are pre-mortem, usually arranged through the soon-to-be-deceased's lawyer.

One of the running jokes about mortuary science (yes, haters, it's a science) is that we all get freaky with the merchandise. Untrue. It's no more than a third of us, at least in my experience. I certainly don't. Dead bodies are rife with communicable diseases. Plus, the smell. Still, just because I don't bend that way doesn't mean I can't accommodate those who do. Money talks, meat doesn't.

***

It started about a year ago. Jennifer Marsh, the It Girl *Instagram* hottie twenty-two-year-old world-beating firecracker whose first nude scene in *Personal Corruption* has been streamed fifty million times on *Mr. Skin* ended up gracing my slab after somebody miscalculated the heroin-fentanyl ratio.

Brain dead at Cedars Sinai after collapsing at a club. She was still pretty fresh when I picked her up. Even I was tempted to ignore the expiration date.

My phone buzzed right after I returned with the body. "Tasteful Departures, Anton speaking."

"Mr. Mack, I'm told you're superintending Jennifer Marsh's final preparations."

"Who is this?"

"I represent Ms. Marsh's biggest fan. This person wants to meet her and is willing to pay."

I looked from side to side, then remembered that I was alone.

"I'm right outside."

I went to the window. A car costing more than everything I'd ever own sat in the drive. A darkened figure holding a phone waved.

We negotiated in the parlour.

He was a lawyer. No name. He always dressed the same: brilliant suit, black balaclava, and black leather gloves. He opened a black leather briefcase and presented the money, one hundred thousand dollars.

"My client requires only an hour with her. My client agrees to wear protection, so there should be no biological residue. All we ask is a private space free of cameras and the smells of your trade."

"Gee, I figured he'd groove on the antiseptics."

The lawyer frowned. "I never disclosed my client's sex."

This was obviously no laughing matter. I palmed my phone and did a quick online search. "You know, California Health and Safety Code section 7052

provides that 'every person who willfully commits...
an act of sexual penetration on, or has sexual contact
with, any remains known to be human, without
authority of law—'"

"'...[I]s guilty of a felony.'" My client is well-
advised regarding the possible legal consequences
of this request. And the health risks involved.

"She's been autopsied."

He smiled. "Even better."

I shuddered. "One hour."

"One hour. Moreover, you must accompany
me in this parlour during that time. My client
demands privacy."

I smiled. "Done."

He frowned, then slid me the money.

I held out my hand. He wouldn't shake it.

***

After it was over, and right before they left, I made
a suggestion. "You know, I get a lot of, well, celebrity
traffic. I don't know how regularly your client—"

His smile belied his reply. "This, I assure you, was
a one off."

"Of course it was."

He rose to leave, then turned and waved his
fingers. "Keep them cold . . . but not too cold."

***

The lawyer rang again two weeks later, this time for Mimi Madrigal, fortysomething former porn star whose cam shows and stripping engagements afforded her a nice bungalow in Studio City. DUI. Missing limb.

Again, we sat in my parlour.

"The crash severed her left arm."

"My client understands that."

"I assume that means you want a discount."

"No, that's unnecessary. However, this time, I'm representing more than one interested party."

"Oh?"

"So, given my fiduciary obligations to those parties—"

"You wanna group rate."

"Well, something like that."

"How many?"

"Three."

"Domes or no?"

"One of them desires to proceed unprotected. So—"

"Two-fifty."

"Two."

"Two twenty-five, and I'll clean up."

"You already clean up. But, okay."

***

After that, it became a regular thing. I cut in colleagues handling in-demand product. One of the clients even splurged for a VIP room. Some of them grooved on the mortuary thing. Some of them wanted to pretend otherwise.

***

Things changed right after I picked up Lana Oaks, formerly America's favourite mom, whose ALS battle celebrity gossip sites chronicled in fawning, if clinical, detail until a co-morbid heart condition claimed her. The conversation about her salability went as you might expect.

"ALS isn't contagious, right?"

"Nope."

"Disfiguring?"

"Not in her case. And, bonus points, no autopsy because cause of death is known."

"Would you give her a Y-scar anyway? I mean, after the clients who don't want one have had their turn?"

Anyway, things went normally, as normally as normal can be in these circumstances. I went in to tidy up and discovered that other, unpurchased meat had been propped up and arranged around Lana's now-besmirched remains, corpse voyeurs.

The lawyer put a hand on my shoulder from behind. I was livid. "This isn't in the contract!"

"Apologies. Some of the clients kink harder than others. Will another twenty thousand cover the damage?"

One of the audience stiffs slipped forward. Then its Y-incision reopened. Guts spilled onto the floor.

"Jesus Christ!"

The lawyer was unmoved. "Thirty thousand?"

"Are you kidding me?"

Then he got nasty. The menace in his voice was measured but unmistakable. "Mr. Mack, remember your place. You work for us now. As far as I'm concerned, giving you any more money is gratuitous. This place is a disgusting supermarket of death. Whether my clients make it a little more disgusting is irrelevant. So, take the money, smile, and be goddamned grateful."

He held out a bundle of cash. I took it.

***

As a rule, addictions gradually demand bigger risks for the same rewards. My clients' needs proved no exception.

It started with a tragic (or maybe not so tragic) bus crash. The cast of *Sparkling Secrets*, a musical on ice, perished. Nationwide mourning. Or celebration, because fate struck a blow for good taste.

Anyway, my clients wanted to fuck them.

The lawyer persisted despite my cautions.

"Dude, it was a bus crash. Gnarly shit. I've reconstructed a bunch of bus crashers. It's instant boner death."

"My clients disagree."

"Plus, they're all at County."

"Do you know someone there?"

"I know almost everybody there."

"Well, then, it's only a matter of money."

"Let me feel them out."

"Please do so promptly. Expiration dates, you know."

Don't I.

***

It wasn't a conversation one has over the phone.

I drove to the county morgue. Lucky for me, Groomer, one of the medical assistants, was on duty. Don't ask why we call him that. All stringy hair, sleeve tattoos, and sketch, he smoked near the loading dock beside a sign demanding he do so thirty yards away.

Ah, the things we make other people do for love.

"Hey boss."

"Hey."

"Got a delivery?"

I looked up at the camera above us.

"Is that on?"

He smiled. "Nope. It's been out for weeks. That's why I can smoke out here."

I exhaled. "I have a special request."

He smiled, too knowingly. "*Sparkling Secrets*?"

"How did you—"

"Dude, this is L.A."

"You're right. Stupid question."

"My clients want a full review."

"That'll cost."

"How much?"

"Sixty. A piece. That includes clean-up."

"For how long?"

"One hour."

"Done."

"And I can't stagger them. Sorry. We get busy."

I smiled. "So do they."

***

Six clients appeared, plus the lawyer. The clients wore baggy track suits, hoodies, gloves, and masks. The lawyer approached. "My clients must be assured your surveillance is disabled."

Groomer smiled. "But of course."

***

Groomer slipped the security guard twenty thousand. He disconnected all the cameras and went to get burgers. Then the clients entered.

One of them stopped, approached me, and pinched my cheeks. She spoke with an endearing lilt. "*Somebody's* going to Hell!"

The lawyer smiled. She then released me and joined the others. Groomer, the lawyer, and I remained outside.

Groomer smoked weed.

"You know, I should have brought nachos. Next time, I'll have to bring nachos."

Groomer smiled. "Nachos sound boss."

The lawyer turned to us.

"Nachos?

"Don't you like nachos?"

"That's not my point."

"Hey, Morrison."

We looked up.

Edgar Spence, the Medical Examiner, approached.

Morrison was Groomer's real name.

"Smoking again? That shit'll kill you."

He noticed the lawyer and me. "Who're your friends?"

"Um-"

He looked at the lawyer's balaclava. "And why are you—"

The muscle the lawyer hired to deter interlopers sprung from some bushes and felled the ME. Then he carried him inside. We followed.

The orgy was full-blown. Fifteen musical skaters in various states of mutilation and fornication. Two clients bickered over a gorgeous female, perfect besides being headless.

"Dude, I was here first."

"We're all 'here.'"

"Do you have any idea who I am?"

"No. You're wearing a mask."

"Okay. Fifty K, me to you, to go first."

"A hundred."

"A hundred!"

"Hey, you can't put a price on love."

The lawyer interrupted them. "Hey people. Sorry to be coitus interruptus. We have an interloper."

The goon hoisted the ME for effect.

The lawyer smiled. "Who wants to kill him?"

Groomer blanched. "Dude! What?!"

The lawyer turned to him, pointing a silenced pistol. "And this one."

I said nothing.

The lawyer turned to me. "There's a crematory here, right?"

"Yes."

"And you can operate it?"

"Yes."

"Then we're good."

One of the guys formerly arguing over headless hottie raised his hand. "I wanna do it."

The lawyer smiled. "Why not?"

Groomer regarded me with horror. "Dude! Do something!"

The lawyer pistol whipped him. He dropped.

Then he smiled at me. "Like he said. Do something."

***

Two hours later, Groomer and the ME were dead. Every medical implement on site had been misused upon them. The lawyer forbade the clients from keeping souvenirs. They booed when it was time to burn the remains.

***

I don't believe in God. And my moral boundaries are obviously porous. Still, I couldn't abide what was supposed to happen next.

My phone rang. It was the lawyer.

"Yup."

"Mr. Mack."

"Counsellor."

"A very special client has a very special order."

"When you put it that way, it sounds like you're staging an intervention to get me off cocaine."

"Ha."

"We going to need to warm things up."

"Do you want me to install a heat lamp?"

"Ha. No. He wants the flower right after it's been picked."

My guts tightened.

He hummed the opening of a song I'd heard on the radio. I strained to recall it.

"Anyway, the client wants to watch you autopsy her."

"Okay."

"While she's still alive. I believe the technical term for this is 'vivisection.'"

"You're asking me to kill her."

He mocked me. "Oh, no! Infamy reigns! Angels weep!"

He was fuck-you firm. "You're already an accessory after the fact to two murders, and even a slow-witted prosecutor could probably hang you for felony murder, too. 'Amor fati,' as Nietzsche said. Plus, we'll pay you half a million dollars. Buy stuff until your conscience doesn't matter."

I said nothing.

"Is that a 'yes' I hear? Good. I'll call with the details tomorrow."

***

Amor fati. Ha. The song the lawyer had hummed came on the radio while I reconstructed the face of a soccer mom who did the PCH on sertraline and merlot. It was Priscilla Keen's *My Body, My Rules*. Ha.

Finding where she lived didn't take long. *Crib Def*, a celebrity fan site, had profiled her five-million-dollar Malibu spread three weeks ago. I downloaded all her music and played it in the car on the way over, hoping that I liked it enough to keep going and that I didn't hate it so much that I'd stop.

I drove up to a huge gate, got out, and approached the security box.

"Help you?"

"Hi, I'm here to see Ms. Keen."

"You're not on the schedule."

"Tell her I'm here because someone's going to try to kill her."

"Seriously? If this is bullshit, we have friends in LAPD. They'll make sure you have a bumpy ride."

"I'm serious."

The gate opened.

***

Two guys frisked me in the atrium, a lovely confluence of Italian marbles and fresh flowers that felt like a mausoleum.

I met her in the living room just as impressive as it was on *Crib Def*.

"So, somebody wants to murder me?"

I turned around. So did the guard assigned to me. "Yes."

She was perfect, hands on hips, wearing only a bikini.

"Did you go to the cops?"

"No. I—"

"Good."

"Good?"

"Good."

"Why is that good?"

"Because that simplifies things. Right, Kimbrough?"

A familiar voice. "Right."

I turned. It was the lawyer. I hadn't seen his face, but his voice was unmistakable.

Someone behind me stuck a syringe in my neck. I staggered, then collapsed on the couch.

The lawyer loomed above me. "Well, this is morally irregular for you, Mr. Mack. After things got unplanned the other night, I feared that we might have lost you. So, we designed this test."

"Test?"

Priscilla smiled and lit a cigarette. "Yup. Fail."

The lawyer looked at her. "Think anyone will pay to fillet?"

She scrutinized me. "Not pretty enough. But Dim Sum will hit anything if you get enough coke in him."

I faded out.

Priscilla crouched beside me and pinched my cheeks.

Once again, that endearing lilt. "*Somebody's* going to Hell!"

EVERYBODY COMES FIRST

The waiting area was pimp palatial: luxe leather chairs, real palm trees, and three million dollars of surprisingly tasteful modern art. Health and Human Services' fifty-million-dollar interior design budget attracted congressional oversight, but, as usual, to no avail. I sat down in one of the chairs, and goddamned was it comfy. I knew I'd have to stand again. But not right now.

An informational video ran across from me: A pig-tailed munchkin smiled heart-meltingly from her hospital bed. "Hi. I'm Christy. I like colouring, playing with my friends, and horses. Especially horses. In case you didn't notice, I'm in the hospital. You know how chocolate chip cookies aren't quite ready if you don't cook them long enough? Well, that's how I came out of Mommy. Not quite ready."

The feed cut to Christy feeding a pony. Then came the soothing voiceover. "Christy was born three months premature and faced numerous medical challenges. Her doctors feared she'd never live a normal life. But breakthroughs in medical technology and the abundance of donated organs made available through Health and Human Services' recently implemented TermCare initiative have brought hope to Christy and her family."

The feed cut to Christy and Mikey, her seven-year-old brother, colouring. Mikey smiled winningly at the camera. "Christy just got a new liver. The one she was born with didn't work right. The new one works as good as mine!"

Christy playfully threw a crayon at him. "It works even better!"

Both then smiled at the camera. "Everybody comes first!"

An amiable receptionist approached and leaned over me, putting her hands between her knees. The condescension was palpable.

"May I help you, sir?"

I smiled.

"Are you a patient? This is an administrative office, but I can direct you to a patient services facility."

***

TermCare was short for "Terminal Care," more popularly known as "Kill Care." Quote Universal healthcare is the hallmark of a civilized society unquote. And so, in 2022, the federal government socialized medicine. The initiative was called "Wellness Federal," "WellFed" for short. Opponents predicted long waits, widespread incompetence, and financial ruin, none of which came to be. WellFed was solvent and efficient, mostly because, as WellFed's bureaucratic overseers might put it, traditional roadblocks to self-monetization were smoothed.

I'm seventy. I have Stage 4 lung cancer. Not a smoker, just unlucky. My doctor admitted me to a WellFed OncoCare facility for treatment. Lots of saccharine faces: everybody's a warrior, we've got your back, typical American can-do bullshit. But the first person I saw wasn't a treatment coordinator. It was one of the TermCare Ambassadors WellFed sicced on the terminally and/or expensively ill to get them to surrender to social utility. We called them "Termites." She was pretty and professional, smiley and charming, and too enthusiastic. "Mr. Dobkins?"

"Right here."

"Hi, I'm Mindy. I'm a WellFed TermCare Ambassador."

She held out a hand. I declined to shake it. "That's a mouthful."

She persisted. "I know you might have heard negative rumours about our program, but, really, I'm here to help. You're under no obligation to avail yourself of any of the services I'm here to discuss. My mandate is simply to educate you about your options. Choice is the hallmark of WellFed's mission."

"I'm sure."

I relented, then shook her hand. "Okay, spin it up."

She sat beside me. "Are you comfortable?"

"Frankly, no."

She chuckled. "I guess I had that coming."

She glanced at the tablet computer she'd brought. "Stage 4 lung cancer. I'm so sorry."

I thought about crying. Maybe that would put her off balance. Then again, it might prompt them to sedate me.

Her voice tone perfectly mixed sympathy and enthusiasm. "Let me throw a number at you."

"Okay.

"Eight hundred fifty thousand dollars."

"What's that?"

"That's the estimated price tag for giving you eight to fourteen more months."

"Are you a doctor?"

"No, but your participation in WellFed implies your consent to allow me access to your files."

"Participation is mandatory."

She smiled, unfazed. "So, eight hundred fifty thousand dollars."

She smiled through the awkward implications.

"You're not going to pay it?"

"Of course we're going to pay it. If that's what you elect. But before you commit to care, let's talk about how we, or should I say you, might better spend that money."

"Instead of on saving my life?"

"Instead of only extending your life a few months at the expense of freedom and dignity."

"Okay, how much do I get?"

"Three hundred and fifty thousand."

"What about the rest?"

"Part goes to your maintenance care. Part to your final arrangements. The rest get reinvested in WellFed."

"How much do you get?"

"Me?"

"Yeah, you. I hear Termites drive flashy."

She smiled, still unfazed. "We're not predators. A world-class team of ethicists created our praxis protocols. Profit motives contradict those protocols."

I sighed. "Okay, what can I do with it—the money."

"Whatever you like, as long as it's legal. We find that many clients go on extended vacations. But if you're thinking of flying to another country and seeking treatment there, I wouldn't. We have medical extradition treaties with all the ones you'd want to visit. And the others don't offer anything resembling what we'd call medicine. It's more like witchcraft."

"Witchcraft?"

She was suddenly nervous. "Not that I'm disparaging Wiccans or their practices, which have a long and valid history of religious identity and expression."

I chuckled. She regained her footing. "What we encourage people to do is invest and, to the extent they are able, participate in WellFed-approved charities. Like our juvenile diabetes foundation. Or our various literacy efforts."

"What if I want to give it to cats?"

"That's cool, too. Animals America is a WellFed TermCare Charitable Partner."

"Gambling? Whores?"

"Well, yes, but there are conditions."

"Conditions?"

"Conditions. Expenditure of TermCare resources for gambling, sex, or drugs is taxed at sixty percent. Besides, WellFed discourages clients from patronizing sex workers because sex work undermines human rights undergirding overall social wellness."

"But it's my money."

"Actually, it's everybody's money, and we've found it best to discourage spending it on antisocial activities. And, is that what you want your legacy to be? I mean, we like to think of this program as a way for you to become your best self through others. A kind of immortality, if you like."

"By dying quicker."

"By liberating social resources for optimal utilization."

"Jesus, do you people speak English?"

"Sorry. What I'm saying is this: How do you want people to remember you? As a crass hedonist chasing fleeting pleasures?"

"Maybe."

Another pause.

"I should tell you that we're running a special this month."

"A special?"

"A special."

"Aren't specials kind of, well, crass?"

She frowned, however slightly. "If you direct all of your OptionCare savings to one of our approved charities, your name will be engraved in the onyx memorial adorning the lobby of our offices in DC. And your remains will be eligible for inclusion in our Arlington memorial garden."

I exhaled. "This is a lot to process. Can I get a beer?"

"I'm sorry, but for liability reasons, clients are disallowed alcoholic beverages on WellFed property."

"What?"

She laughed. "Of course you can have a beer! We have a lounge downstairs. Would you like me to accompany you?"

***

I sat alone. The beer, Belgian and hoppy, helped purge some of the nonsense. The chair was leather, cushy, comfy. An oil portrait on one wall memorialized the guy whose TermCare buyout funded the lounge. Or that's what the plaque beneath it said. I wasn't sure whether to toast him or pity him.

I didn't see her coming.

"Mr. Dobkins." Before me was a slight, severe nurse. "Don't believe them."

"Who?"

"The Termites." She handed me a business card. Written on it was a phone number. Nothing else.

"Mr. Dobkins?" I turned. It was Mindy. Before her was a little boy in a wheelchair.

The nurse departed. I pocketed the card.

"Mr. Dobkins, I'd like you to meet somebody." The boy waved, beaming.

I downed the beer. Then I rose and crouched before the boy, my hands between my knees.

"Who are you?"

"I'm Rodge."

I shook his hand.

"Wanna beer, Rodge?"

Mindy smiled. She knew I was kidding.

"Rodge is here because he needed new lungs. And, thanks to the charity of someone who wanted to give life to the next generation, he got them. Now he can play soccer."

"And baseball!"

"And baseball."

I put a hand on his shoulder. "Play as much as you can before you get old, son. And use up those lungs before they try to take 'em back."

I smiled at a now-horrified Mindy. "I'll be in touch."

***

I went to my favourite bar. Hal, the bartender, let me drink as much as I wanted (screw WellFed's two-drink-a-day maximum). After my third beer, I called the number on the card.

The nurse answered. "Yes?"

"We met in the lounge earlier today."

"Yes. Where are you?"

"Charleton's at Third and Broad."

"See you in ten."

***

Her name was Barbara Crabbe. She was a WellFed oncology nurse. And she was a little too earnest and prophetic. "I don't have a lot of time."

"Okay."

"You're never going to get treatment."

"What?"

"You're too old, too sick, and therefore too expensive."

"They can't just deny me treatment."

"They will."

"They said they wouldn't."

"They'll find a way. Look, if you don't believe me, tell Mindy you want treatment. Then watch what happens. When you realize I'm right, call me again."

She looked at her watch, rose, and departed.

***

Mindy was again too enthusiastic, like a theme park guide. "Hey, Mr. Dobkins!"

"Hello."

"So, what did you decide?"

"I'm gonna fight this."

"That's definitely an option." She pulled out the tablet and pecked at it nervously.

"So…"

"So, there's a vetting process."

"What do you mean?"

"You're beyond the mandatory treatment parameters."

"What are those?"

"WellFed clients experiencing ailments exceeding typical age and morbidity parameters are automatically re-evaluated for treatment eligibility."

A youngish man in a suit appeared. Like Mindy, he was blandly officious. "Mr. Dobkins?"

"Yes."

"I'm Connor. I'm—"

"You look like a lawyer."

"I am. WellFed assigned me to review your care petition. All clients seeking extraordinary care must be vetted for social and ethical integrity."

"I don't understand."

"We've reviewed your last five federal income tax filings and found some irregularities we need to investigate before approving your treatment."

"What irregularities?"

"You should retain counsel before we discuss them. Moreover, I should tell you that, if we do find misconduct on your part, you're liable for the cost of my services along with any penalties you might face. Now, given your age and diagnosis, we're willing to forgo this review if you agree simply to waive treatment and take the TermCare payment Mindy offered you yesterday. In fact, if you do, you won't be billed for the time I've expended on your case thus far."

"And if I fight this, if I get a lawyer—"

"We'd expedite the inquiry, but it could take up to six months."

"What?!"

"There's also the matter of your drinking problem. Substance abuse issues typically disqualify clients from extraordinary treatment protocols."

"Drinking problem?"

"Charleton's, the tavern you frequent, is notorious for flouting WellFed alcohol consumption laws."

I felt faint. Then I heard a familiar voice. "C'mon, Dad. Why are you fighting this?"

I turned to see my son, Niles, and his family. They'd just entered Mindy's office. I hadn't seen them for almost a year.

"Who invited you?"

Mindy called us.

"Doesn't that violate my privacy rights?"

Mindy smiled. "Not if you evidence inability properly to administer your affairs."

"Dad, she's really worried about you. That you're going to make the wrong decision."

"The wrong decision?"

"Dad, we're so sorry about your diagnosis, but, when it's time, it's time. And, I mean, don't you want Maisie to go to college?"

Maisie was my endlessly adorable granddaughter. Her face crinkled. "Pop-Pop doesn't want me to go to college?"

Colleen, my barely tolerable daughter-in-law, comforted Maisie. "Of course not, honey."

Niles glared at me. "Right, Dad?"

Mindy smiled. "If you use your TermCare payment to endow Maisie's higher education fund, the Department of Education will guarantee a dollar-for-dollar matching payment."

"Dad, that would cover grad school, too. You know how much Maisie wants to be a doctor."

Maisie hugged my legs. "Please, Pop-Pop! Please!"

***

It was all too much. I caved, assigning the payout to Maisie's fund. They promised me they wouldn't go after Hal, but a few days later I discovered Charleton's shuttered pending an alcoholic beverage control investigation. I collapsed on the bench outside. After composing myself, I called Niles. It went to voicemail. He preferred to text, but his replies to my texts were sporadic at best. I called Nurse Crabbe.

As I hung up, I heard a vehicle approach. "Mr. Dobkins?" It was Mindy. She drove an absurd SUV, all leather, chrome, and rims.

"Nice ride."

She smiled, bubbly. "How are you doing?"

"I'm dying of cancer."

She handed me a card.

"What's this?"

She smiled sincerely. "WellFed has free services for clients seeking to end their suffering. They'll even come to your home!"

"Suicide, huh?"

She paused. "Look, it's pull or be pulled. And where's the dignity in being pulled?"

I rose and handed the card back. She frowned. "What are you going to do?"

"I'm going to use the balance of my Social Security check to pay a couple strippers to defile each other. Would you like to join me?"

She frowned and sped off.

"That was funny."

I turned around. Nurse Crabbe was behind me. "Wanna put your stripper money to better use?"

"I'm not sure that stripper money has a better use."

She smiled and took my arm. "Humour me."

***

The receptionist persisted. "Sir, are you experiencing a medical crisis? Would you like me to call an ambulance?"

They all spoke the same bloodless language. They all had this lifeless affect. Always rational. Always calm. Always grammatically correct.

An explosion thundered nearby.

We looked up.

The receptionist frowned. "What was that?"

There was another, slightly closer. The receptionist freaked. "Oh my God!"

I looked up at the television. Niles and Maisie smiled at me. It was a WellFed propaganda video about how my sacrifice would allow Maisie to be a doctor. In the last shot, Maisie wore a kid-sized doctor's coat and brandished a toy stethoscope. "Everybody comes first!"

Except me. And because Maisie's education fund wasn't one of WellFed's preferred charities, no onyx memorial or Arlington internment. I smiled at the panicky receptionist. Nurse Crabbe was right. My stripper money was better spent. At least this way.

I stood and opened my jacket. The receptionist recoiled.

The clacker felt right in my hand. The bomb vest was snug but still comfortable.

"What are you doing?"

"Coming first."

SWATTED

It was an unremarkable house on an unremarkable street in an unremarkable town. We got tipped a drug dealer was lamming within. Multiple warrants, a good get if we got him: Citations, maybe even promotions. Getting the night-time, no-knock, SWAT warrant was easy because our favourite judge was on call. You could be dressed like Lady Gaga and tripping balls and he'd still sign off.

He smiled at the application. "Another night-time incursion."

"We prefer they don't see us coming."

"Ooooh. Multiple warrants. Your friend's quite the miscreant."

"He's not our friend."

The Judge grinned even wider, then signed the warrant. "Nor is he mine. Happy hunting."

***

It was me, Rodge, Jorge, and Rinley, our Squad Commander. We came dark (no sirens or emergency lights). Supporting officers quietly evacuated neighbouring homes while my other team members took up surveillance points around the subject property. Once the supporting officers secured the neighbours, Jorge fired flashbangs through the front windows. Rodge and I rammed the front door, shields in front, M-4s right behind. No call out. I mean, if the suspected drug dealers inside (every house contains suspected drug dealers, didn't you know?) heard us announce themselves, they'd destroy contraband (they always have contraband).

Three officer-involved shootings later, the house was clear.

The most important lesson you learned when you shot someone in the line of duty is that you were always in fear for your life. Even when you weren't. Even when you obviously shouldn't have been. In this case, we were. Or at least I was. Though I'm not sure I should have been.

Dad brandished a baseball bat; Jorge took him out. He was probably disoriented from the flashbangs; that's what they're designed to do. Jorge told him to drop it. He didn't. Of course, flashbangs can also cause temporary deafness. Department procedures don't account for that. Lucky us. Mom attacked Jorge from behind after watching him down Dad. Jorge downed her. She attacked a cop, knowingly. That Jorge shot her husband right in front of her was irrelevant.

I got suspect number three on floor number two. I ordered him to freeze. He bolted, terrified. There was something in his hand. It was a phone. He'd been calling 911. He was only fifteen.

***

Standard protocol: grand jury review. But, before that, before we wrote the incident reports, and before the department-ordered counselling, we met with June, the Deputy County Attorney who was going to present the case. The County Attorney and Chief were on the same page about whether cops ever shot the wrong people, and that page said they didn't, even when they did. June was slight and wispy, but clearly kicked ass. Bonus points: She was a badge bunny, and currently fucking Jorge.

We sat in the squad room while she explained how it was to, ahem, go down. The Chief watched from one corner. We had enforced his protocols, and he wasn't about to see us fry for it.

June smiled. "I've got a perfect no-bill record and I don't want you screwing that up."

The Chief nodded. "Amen."

The unit traded smiles.

"Okay. There's good news and bad news. The bad news is that the house was clean. No drugs, no drug paraphernalia, not even a bootleg DVD. Now, I'm not saying that you should ever plant evidence. In fact, as an officer of the court, I'd say that you should never plant evidence. That would be both illegal and highly unethical. But if some contraband had been found in the house, things would be better for you."

Jorge interrupted her. "Well, what's the good news?"

The Chief stepped in. "The good news is that your intel wasn't total crap. Your target was at the house. Two days ago. The mom was her cousin, and, apparently, she booted him an hour after he arrived."

"So?"

June smiled. "So, why didn't she dime him out? I mean, that's what a good citizen does, blood or no blood, right? Now she goes from blameless victim of quote police overkill unquote to aider-and-abettor of wanted felon."

"How do we know she knew he had warrants?"

"Who cares?"

We grinned darkly.

***

It worked: No bill. Bonus points: The family apparently had no relations looking to sue for wrongful death. More good news: The state's sunshine laws don't apply to unindicted public servants. No angry phone calls. No crusading reporters. Just business as usual.

***

The shrink the department makes you visit when you cap somebody seemed unmoved when I told her all this. There was a metronome clicking back and forth on a table adjacent her. She said it helped her patients concentrate.

"You said no one's suing?"

"Not that I know of. I mean, apparently, they don't have any relatives. I mean, you'd figure somebody would pop up for a quick settlement. Relatives are less annoying when you can cash them out."

"That's pretty dark."

"So's my job.

"You shot a kid. What do you think about that?"

"I think I did my job."

She frowned. "Your job is—"

"I think it's horrible. But I thought he had a gun. I mean, I think it's funny that they ask you to armchair my life or death. Even with training, you've got, like, half a second to figure shit out. Ask Rodge. Ask Jorge. They'll tell you the same. You talked to them, right?"

"I can't say. Therapist-patient privilege."

"Well, that's what they'd say."

She sighed, then smiled. "I just want to see how you're processing all this."

"I'm processing it."

The metronome kept clicking. Tick-tock, tick-tock, tick-tock.

***

It happened about a week later. Night-time call. Another forgettable house on another forgettable street, suddenly not so forgettable. Shots fired. Screams. We didn't even need the Judge; SWAT response was standard in these cases. It was an upscale colonial house at the end of cul-de-sac. No nearby neighbours. We established a perimeter. Jorge sent in the flashbangs. Rodge and I stormed in, Rinley behind us.

Rodge shouted. "GUN! GUN! GUN!"

I crouched, gun pointed. Jorge drew a bead and fired. My ears rang. The perp, standing above us on a second-floor balcony overlooking the front door, hit the wall and dropped. Jorge and I charged the stairs while Rodge and Rinley covered us. I saw the perp's feet, then the blood smear on the wall behind him.

Jorge ID'ed him first. "Uh-oh."

"What?"

Then I did. "Uh-oh."

The bad news was it was the Judge. The good news was he had a gun in his hand. A .357 magnum. Serious hardware. But I wasn't sure that was going to matter.

"This ain't good. We shot the Judge."

"He had a gun."

"Of course he had a gun!"

Our radios crackled. It was Dispatch. "Alpha Squad. Is your location secure?"

Rinley responded. "Alpha Squad, Squad Commander here. Suspect is down. We're secure. Awaiting forensics and coroner."

"Confirmed. Alpha Squad, we need you to respond ASAP to Madison and Tenth. Officer in need of assistance."

"Dispatch, what about OIS protocols—"

"Executive override is in effect! You're cleared to go!"

We went. We left the Judge for the forensics guys. And, mindful of DCA June's injunction never to plant evidence on a dead suspect, I did not slip a vial of Colombian Happytime into his robe's front pocket. Americans don't do nuance; here, you're either Jesus or Satan. Better still, nobody's ever sure which one you are. Till they are, at least. So, a beloved public servant is actually a reckless cokehead rightfully gunned down in his home.

***

Madison and Tenth was half a mile away, and the streets were mostly quiet. Only our siren and lights disturbed the night. As we approached the intersection, it was hard to process what we saw, even though it was pretty clear what was happening. There was a squad car. Fully aflame. Three figures before it.

We parked and exited, M-4s brandished, and approached the scene. The fire shadowed the figures. I saw only outlines at first.

Rinley keyed his radio. "Dispatch, Alpha Squad. Responding to Madison and Tenth."

We drew close enough at last to see. It was some ghastly shit.

Rinley was on the radio again. "Dispatch, we've got officers down!"

Two officers down, a perp kneeling between them in their mixing blood. The perp tore one officer's face off and started eating.

We all fired at once. No warning, no hesitation. The perp flew apart.

We reloaded, then approached.

"What the—"

The perp's head had rolled beside one the squad car's flattened tires. Her face was unmistakable in the firelight. A chunk of flesh still hung from her mouth. It was June.

Jorge appeared unmoved.

"Oh my God."

The vics' faces had been eaten off. I couldn't bring myself to check their vitals.

Rodge puked beside them.

Rinley fell to his knees. His radio barked. "Alpha Squad, Dispatch. Command requests update."

Rinley puked. Then he keyed his radio. "Alpha Squad, Dispatch. Come in, please."

Rodge's phone rang. He answered it.

Rinley wiped his mouth, then responded. "Dispatch, Alpha Squad. Officers down, repeat, officers down. We need a bus. I mean—"

Rodge shot him. Full auto. His head exploded. Rodge then turned towards Jorge, but Jorge fired first. Rodge's armour caught the burst. Rodge fired back. Jorge's helmet skittered on the pavement behind him, half his head inside.

"RODGE!"

He regarded me blankly, smiled, then emptied the mag under his chin.

***

I sat in the squad room before the Chief and the County Attorney. I hadn't even showered. Blood and puke splattered my gear.

The Chief paced. "What the fuck happened out there?!"

I couldn't stop looking down at my feet.

"Officer!"

I looked up. "I don't know. Rodge just lost it. He killed Rinley, then Jorge, then himself."

The County Attorney pounced. "But not you!"

I smiled weakly. "Nope."

The Chief frowned. "Stop smiling!"

"Who shot my Deputy?"

"We did. I mean Alpha Squad."

"All of you?"

I nodded.

"Why?"

"She was eating…"

"What do you mean she was eating?"

"Their faces…"

"Whose faces?"

"She was kneeling between two downed officers, in front of their burning squad car, and eating their faces."

"What?"

"That's what we saw. That's why we fired."

They didn't believe it.

"Well, technically, we only saw her eating one of the faces. My guess is she downed the other one before we arrived."

My phone buzzed. I ignored it. The call went to voicemail.

It buzzed again.

I answered. It was the shrink.

***

Cannibalism is a sometime side effect of indulging bath salts. And June had enough in her system to space a cinder block. Jorge dosed her a few hours before our encounter. She went on a killing spree culminating in the face-eating buffet and firing squad. Jorge didn't know what he was doing. Neither did Rodge. And neither did I when I drew my service weapon and capped the Chief and the County Attorney. I'm guessing as much, at least.

She had counselled all of us after the attack.

I kept hearing the metronome, dull and relentless, as I recalled the shrink explaining that the boy I shot was her nephew and no one knew because she'd been adopted as a kid. She'd recently re-connected with her sister, the mom Rodge shot for attacking Jorge. And all I knew was that I would do whatever she wanted, whenever she asked, not matter how much I didn't want to.

Like swatting the Judge.

And shooting these idiots.

And shooting myself.

Tick-tock, tick-tock, tick-tock.

A GOOD SCARE

The shrink was disputing my judgment. I took this to be a good sign.

"Tell me again why you want to do this."

"I love a good scare."

"That's a bullshit response. This is more than just a good scare. The fact you're even requesting it arguably indicts your judgment."

He sighed. "I've talked to plenty of you. I think you're callused nihilists willing to do any depraved thing to get frizzed. The last person I evaluated for them continually bursts into tears and can't go outside without wearing adult diapers. The one before that sets her hair on fire every time we take off the straitjacket. I fully expect the authorities to shutter this little creep show as a menace to public morals. So, I repeat, tell me again why you want to do this."

"Because you fully expect the authorities to shutter it as a menace to public morals."

He chuckled.

I had no good answer. I could have said I was one of those depraved nihilists indulging vaporous pleasures while waxing fulsome indifference to my wellbeing, but that sounded unhealthy. Still, it didn't matter. He just had to certify that I was sound-minded and capable of consenting to their depredations, which apparently are not mutually exclusive concepts. And I was.

***

Undertaken is an extreme haunted house attraction near Chicago. I was three years on the waiting list and got called after the woman in front of me choked to death buffet bingeing. They asked if I was superstitious and wanted to pass. I said it made things even cooler. They agreed.

Undertaken was mostly secret. I knew only that its tactics were primarily psychological. I mean, anybody could waterboard you and make you eat scorpions. The real genius of scary, at least to me, was surprising you with yourself, with what you thought you knew all along, warping reality along the way.

***

There were three of us. Me, Jonah Fox, who wrote for *horror4evrr.com*, and Megan Caldwell, a horror movie fanatic who, like me, wanted a good scare. A limousine dropped us before a Victorian rambler encircled by wrought iron. The untamed front lawn crept through the bars.

Jonah marvelled. "Dude, I think this place might be real. I mean, real real."

We passed through the elaborate, if decayed, front gate. Inscribed above: "Hell is kinder." The lawn tangled trash and sprung animal traps, rats rotting in their grasp. "Welcome" was written in what I expect was pig's blood on the elaborate front door, which opened with a textbook creepy creak. We entered. The lighting was erratic; formaldehyde tinged the air. A bland guy in a dark three-piece suit approached. He seemed just as likely to be selling frozen yogurt as managing corpses.

"We're so glad you've arrived. We didn't think she'd have any mourners. No one should die unloved."

"What?"

"Now, before we proceed, could you please get against the wall so that I may frisk you for contraband."

Megan paused. "Um—"

"I must insist. Otherwise, you're disallowed from going further and, as you acknowledged in the contract, will be ineligible for a refund."

I got against the wall. He spread my hands and legs, then frisked me. He found nothing. "Good. Congratulations, and welcome."

Jonah carried nothing. But Megan had a phone. Bland Guy dangled it before her judgmentally.

"I'm sorry. I didn't think you'd—"

Then Jekyll went full Hyde. "NO PHONES, NO ID! WHAT IS YOUR GODDAMNED PROBLEM!"

He slapped her, hard, then smashed the phone against the wall. She rose, chastened. We'd agreed to at least some minor violence, but this was pushing it, even for skydive haunters like us.

A little blood dripped from her nose. She licked it and smiled.

Bland Guy lit a massive candelabra and held it aloft. He then opened the doors to the viewing parlour. We entered, giddy. Everything was mahogany trimmed with crimson velvet. Stained glass windows illuminated by the dying sun depicted dead followers of a deader god. Off-key organ music played. Up front was a massive casket. A minister wearing a black veil and inverted cross preached in gibberish from the adjacent podium. He babbled more maniacally as we approached.

The D-squared was a provocatively tattooed, twentysomething hottie. She wore nothing but her Y incision. I was enticed and repulsed. Then I was just enticed.

Bland guy loomed beside us, still wielding the candelabra.

We loomed above her.

I couldn't resist. "Who was she?"

"Someone looking for a thrill. Just like you. Come now, pay your respects."

Jonah smiled. "Mind if I use my—"

D-squared hissed and rose, dead-eyed. She grabbed Jonah, whose delight abated as she ate his throat. Blood fountained. It tasted real.

The minister and music continued.

Bland guy shut the casket on D-squared and latched it.

He regarded me and Megan earnestly. "This is wrong. Really wrong. We have to get out of here."

D-squared pounded from within. The casket shuddered on its stand.

"But—but—"

Jonah was at our feet, pale, bled out. His final breath bubbled the blood near his lips.

The minister shrieked and brandished a hatchet. Then he charged.

Bland guy intercepted him, knocking the hatchet to the floor. He torched the minister's cloak with the candelabra. Aflame, the minister frenzied past us down the aisle. He reached the doors, staggered, and dropped.

Melanie was psyched. "This is AWESOME!"

Bland Guy wasn't. "I'm going to prison." He set the candelabra on an adjacent table, pulled a phone from his jacket, and keyed it. "Hello?! Emergency services?!"

The casket rocked, D-squared pounding and shrieking.

"I need police and an ambulance at 1199 River Street. We've had some deaths. Please hurry! Oh, thank you!!"

We heard approaching sirens almost as soon as he hung up.

"They said they have a police unit in the area. It should be here momentarily."

Melanie examined Jonah. "It's so real. This is definitely the best ever."

I looked Bland Guy. "I don't understand. This is supposed to be—"

"Supposed to be a thrill ride. Sick, but legal."

He frowned towards Jonah. "I'm sorry about your friend."

Melanie was unfazed. "We didn't even know him till twenty minutes ago."

The casket, still shuddering, fell and opened. D-squared spilled out, disoriented, enraged. She charged us. Bland Guy grabbed the minister's hatchet and split her face. D-squared dropped and bled out. "Oh, God. Now I'm really going to prison."

Two cops entered the parlour, guns brandished. "Is everybody okay in here?"

One saw the roasted reverend. "Evidently not."

Bland Guy approached them, hands raised. "Oh, thank you for coming. There's, it's just horrible."

"What the hell is going on here?"

"It's supposed to be haunted house. Fake. For money. And it—"

He sobbed and dropped to his knees.

One of the cops looked at us. "Are the rest of you okay?"

We nodded. He smiled. "Well that's too bad."

He shot bland guy's face, splattering his brains at our feet. Then he fired at us. We ducked and charged through a curtained doorway to our left.

Inside was an embalming chamber. The examination table sported a naked guy, Y-incised, viscera exposed.

Autopsy Guy spoke, his voice flat, weak. "Please help. Someone help."

We reeled.

He tried rising from the table but was restrained at the wrists and ankles.

"Dude, what's going on? Are you part of the show?"

"What show?" He beheld himself. "Oh my God! What did they do?!"

Melanie beamed. "This is the euthanasia sequence!"

"What?"

"Or autopsy. Whatever. We just have to kill this guy to get to the next stage!"

"Next stage?"

"Yeah. This is all fake, remember? I mean, where did the cops go?"

She smiled at Autopsy Guy. "Dude, what's your name?"

"Uh—"

"See, he doesn't know his name. Bad acting! I deserve a discount!" Then she spotted the instruments. "Is that what I think it is?"

"What?"

"It is!" She brandished a metal device formed of two metal prongs, one of which moved along a saw-toothed frame. "A thoracotomy tray!"

"What?"

"Rib spreader! I used to play this video game where I was an ER doc, and it kept booting me because I used the rib spreader on everybody, even if they had the sniffles."

Autopsy Guy struggled against his restraints. "Don't let her! This isn't a joke!"

I blocked her. "Don't! I think it's real!"

"Get the fuck outta my way. I paid to ride, and I'm gonna ride!"

I pushed her away. She dropped the rib spreader and, grinning, grabbed a curved blade from the instrument tray.

She charged me. I didn't even know the bone saw was in my grasp. I activated and pushed it into her abdomen. My hand went into her guts, warm and welcoming, then back through her kidney until she was impaled up to my elbow. Her spine scratched my forearm. The bone saw whirred, spraying gore. We collapsed. I withdrew and rose, blood-soaked. There was no way this was fake. I looked at Autopsy Guy. Dead. I think.

"That was outstanding."

I turned. A guy wearing a headset and holding a clipboard stood behind me in a polo shirt and khaki pants. "Hi. I'm Josh. I'm the intern." He offered a fistful of moist towelette packets. "They're all I could find. I figured you'd want to freshen up."

"What?"

"Oh, you're in shock. That's okay. They said that might happen. Just follow me."

I did. But first, I wiped both hands on his pristine polo shirt. "Whoa, space invasion!"

We entered a cosy sitting room, also crimson and mahogany, leather-bound books on dusty shelves. We faced three Peepsters in leather wing chairs. Orange-yellow lamps hung over us, but not over them; their faces were shadows. A massive, scrumptious buffet abutted them. A server in white loomed over a prime rib, carving knife and fork at the ready.

"Don't let him near the buffet. I don't want hepatitis in my scalloped potatoes."

I looked at Josh. "Hepatitis?"

He smiled meekly. "Yeah. Melanie had hepatitis. Not sure why they let her in. Maybe they were afraid of some kind of lawsuit. Oh, well."

"Hepatitis?"

From the shadowed Peepsters, mockingly: "Surprise!"

"How do you know that?"

Josh seemed slightly embarrassed. "Well, you did give us all your medical records."

Another Peepster chimed in. "Hey, that bone saw bit was Christmas special heinous! Can I give him a tip?"

Josh frowned respectfully. "I wouldn't. It'll probably just disappear when they book him."

"You're bringing the cops in here?"

"No. Not in here, obviously."

"They killed —"

"Not those cops. They're fake. I'm talking about the real cops. For you. I mean, you killed Melanie. For real. No bullshit."

"She was going to kill—"

"No one. The guy on the table was animatronic."

"What about Jonah?"

"Who's Jonah?"

Another Peepster. "Don't worry. I'm sure they'll plead you out to involuntary manslaughter."

I grabbed the intern and menaced him. "Who the fuck are they?"

"Hey, I'm just the intern."

"TELL ME!"

"They—they paid."

"Paid?"

"Paid to watch."

"Watch what?"

From the Peepster Gallery: "You." They chuckled.

I dropped to my knees.

"Oh, there it is! The moment of truth! Is this going in the Memories album? This better be going in the Memories album!"

I vomited, then wiped my mouth.

One of the Peepsters chuckled. "Give him something to eat."

The intern didn't understand. "What?"

"Jail food sucks. Trust me. I sell it." The Peepster called to the carver. "Give him a steak sandwich so he doesn't go away with a completely bad taste in his mouth."

The carver looked up. "Me?"

"Yeah, you, Storm Shadow."

Nervously, he carved.

"Make it generous. And don't forget the horseradish."

He added horseradish to the plate, then started towards me.

"I said a sandwich! That means fucking bread!"

The carver grabbed half a baguette from the table and brought it over. It wasn't till he served me that I noticed he'd brought the carving knife.

I took the sandwich. "Thanks."

I flung the plate. It struck the carver's forehead. He dropped the knife. I retrieved it.

It was effortlessly sharp. I slashed the intern from his pelvis to his sternum, freeing his intestines onto my would-be lunch.

"Oh, shit!"

I frenzied the Peepsters, slashing until the floor was covered with noses, ears, fingers, and wing chair stuffing.

After that, I dropped the knife and attacked the buffet: General Tsao's chicken, garlic mashed potatoes, lobster mac and cheese. It was glorious.

I didn't hear him enter.

"Martin?"

I alerted, mid-chew.

"Martin?"

It was the shrink. "Martin. They said you've had, well, rather a break. I know I was rather terse with you before, but really, I'm here to help."

"The lobster mac is insane."

"I'm sure it is. Martin, the ride's finished. It's time to leave."

"What do you mean?"

He approached. "I mean, it's all going to be okay."

"Maybe for me, but what about them?"

He chuckled. "For them, too."

I speared a chicken breast with the knife and offered it to him. "Chicken limon?"

"Thank you, no."

I bit into it. Capers rolled from it onto the floor. "It's good. I thought it would be dry, but I guess it hasn't been out long enough."

I dropped the chicken, then again to my knees, sobbing. The shrink put a hand on my shoulder. "It's okay, Martin." He crouched beside me. "Remember what you said when I asked you why you wanted to do this?"

I nodded.

"What did you say?"

"I said—I said I wanted a good scare."

He smiled. "Well, I've got good news and bad news."

"What's the bad news?"

"The scares so far have been, well, mediocre. The good news is that they're about to get much better."

He stun-gunned me, and I fell onto the caper-laden body parts.

***

"Dude! Where'd the cops go? I can't believe they just capped Lurch like that! Boom!"

The overhead light was harsh. I couldn't shield my eyes. My wrists were secured to the sides of the table. So were my ankles. My head was in cradle. It was an autopsy theatre. The one I'd been in before.

"Dude! He's awake! It's like *Faces of Death* the Game!"

"Is that what I think it is?"

The other one seized the thoracotomy tray and held it up. "Crackalackalackin'!"

"But you have to split the sternum with a bone saw first, right?"

"NO!"

"Dude, it talks!"

"It's so real!"

"NO! Don't please don't!"

One of them mocked me. "*NO! Please don't!*"

I heard the bone saw whine.

"They'll kill you!"

"Oooh, they'll kill us!"

He smiled sympathetically. Then he put a hand on my shoulder. "Let's hope so, buddy. Let's hope so."

SPRING CHICKENS

Tranquility Estates was a retirement home near downtown, old and creepy despite the fresh paint. We called it "the Tranq." And, as if town planners wanted to put all the forgettable people in one place, the county orphanage where I lived was just up the street. Our keepers and theirs frequently mingled us to create endless family-friendly, greeting-card magic moments. And they got them. Except for the family-friendly.

***

Mr. Carter was my favorite: ninety, in and out of the here and now, and fun to talk to because he said whatever he wanted, no matter who got embarrassed. He rated the female nurses on a ten-point scale and occasionally muttered things that further diminished my waning innocence. Today, like so many other days, he wasn't making sense. Or, he was, and I wasn't following.

"Kent?"

"Yeah, Mr. Carter?"

"Kent?"

"Yeah."

"Tell me, have accepted Satan into your heart?"

"What do you mean?"

"I mean what I said. Have you accepted Satan into your heart?"

I didn't know what to say.

"He'll keep you frisky. Just open yourself up and let 'im in."

A brusque nurse appeared behind his wheelchair. She regarded me sympathetically. "I think Mr. Carter needs a nap."

"Do I?"

"I think so."

Mr. Carter smiled at me as the nurse wheeled him away. He whispered "Satan!" while offering two thumbs up. The nurse, smiling dismissively, shook her head.

***

My friend, Millsy, preferred Rubio "Ruby" Ramirez ("Mr. Ruby," as we called him), an army veteran always talking about his favorite war crimes. One afternoon, near the end of the social hour, Mr. Ruby lamented NATO's decision to ban flamethrowers.

"There's something magical about setting people on fire."

I called to Millsy. "C'mon, Millsy, we gotta go."

"I'll catch up."

"Yeah, he'll catch up. I wanna tell him about cluster bombs. You wanna hear about cluster bombs?"

"Maybe next time. Are you coming?"

"Dude, it's just up the street."

"Okay."

Mr. Zane, the orphanage director, let Millsy stay, likely hoping that Mr. Ruby would persuade him to join the military (and therefore the workforce). I departed with a several other kids I barely knew. So many cycled through the home. No one realized many of us had disappeared over the past year. Not even me.

***

After Millsy didn't show at check-in, I went to Mr. Zane. "Seen Millsy?"

"No. He didn't come back from the Tranq?"

"Nope.

He smiled. "Maybe he stayed for dinner. I think tonight is fat-free mac and cheese. Gotta keep those arteries clear."

"That was hours ago."

He mocked me, hands raised. "Whoa! Curfew police! I thought you guys were friends."

***

Millsy didn't return that night. Or the next day. I went to the Tranq to investigate.

A nurse took me to Mr. Ruby. "You looking for Millsy?"

"Yeah. Have you seen him?"

"Not since he left last night. He stayed for dinner, and we talked about flechette ammunition. Is he missing?"

"I don't know. I mean, sometimes he just bails for a few days and comes back."

He took my arm. "Oh, well, I do hope he returns. Would you like to talk about flechette ammunition?"

"I'm good."

"Okay. But please tell me when Millsy comes back. I find his visits invigorating."

"Uh, sure. Will do."

***

Snooping around was easy because everybody was watching the Showcase Showdown. All my favorite horror movies said start in the basement or the attic. I chose the basement. I checked the laundry, then the storage area, then the boiler room. Nothing.

While I was in the boiler room, two orderlies entered. I hid and waited. They lit up.

"Another one tonight."

"Yeah. *I feel so silky smooth.*"

They laughed.

Their radios chirped: "Mrs. Rowe's eating the goldfish again."

They stomped out the cigarettes and left, locking the door behind them. I was trapped. I know, who makes a boiler room with a one-way lock? Like I said, this place was old, like refrigerator-trapped-little-kid old. Anyhow, I knew somebody would unlock the door eventually. And, if nobody did, I'd call for help and lie about getting lost looking for the bathroom.

***

Night came. Still trapped. And I needed to go to the bathroom. I crept about in the ventilation system, hoping to find a vent to an unlocked room. I heard voices and advanced towards them. I peered through another vent. Below was a concrete space centered by a large, circular concrete bath. Bleach smell made me gag.

"God, they overbleached again."

"Gotta kill the flies. We don't want *Amityville Horror* down here."

Two sets of leather straps hung above the bath.

The second orderly sprayed air freshener liberally. The other coughed.

"God. That's even worse."

I heard an exaggerated sniffing sound.

"They overbleached again."

The orderlies turned. It was Mr. Carter. The nurse who'd escorted him away from me pushed his chair. He wore a white bathrobe. Several other residents, also white-robed, clustered behind him.

Three more orderlies, also in white, approached from the side. The middle one carried a white-shrouded figure, the left one a ladder. In a well-practiced routine, two orderlies set up the ladder. The other shouldered the figure and ascended the ladder while the others held it. Upon reaching the top, the orderly grabbed a set of straps and secured them around the figure's feet. He then removed the shroud and released the figure.

It was Millsy. He wore only his boxer shorts. Intra-arterial lines dangled his arms and legs.

Mr. Carter sprung from the chair and disrobed. "Me first!"

He entered the bath. The others doffed their robes and joined him.

The orderly atop the ladder took Millsy's hand and pulled him over. He then released the tourniquets on each line. The blood drizzled. The Bathorites smiled. One of them sponged himself with a loofa. The others bathed each other and talked about, well, anything else.

"Is there any acid?"

"My grandson likes setting fires."

"Do you think the porridge is bland enough?"

***

I escaped through a vent in a ground floor storage room. Town was only a couple miles; I sprinted the whole way. The police station had a twenty-four-hour duty officer.

I told him everything. He laughed in my face. Then he called the orphanage. Mr. Zane arrived fifteen minutes later in the orphanage van.

As he drove, I told him what I told the cop. "They didn't believe me."

"Of course they didn't. I mean, it's seriously crazy."

I sighed, defeated.

"Hey, cheer up."

"What? Why?"

He turned and smiled. "I believe you."

Then he stun-gunned me.

***

I awoke dangling, dazed. Beneath me was the bath, still slick with Millsy's blood.

"Hurry up. We didn't sedate this one."

Nearby, Mr. Zane schmoozed a Tranq administrator. They smiled as a fresh batch of residents scrambled to the tub. Tubes hung from my arms and thighs. An indifferent orderly reached toward me from the ladder.

I regarded him in terror. "Oh, crap. It's awake."

The orderly brandished a scalpel and grabbed my arm. I jerked away, and he fell, smashing his head on the side of the tub. Everybody recoiled while he shuddered and bled.

"Okay. Now it's definitely ruined."

Another orderly was already scaling the ladder, a knife in his teeth. Yeah, it was actually in his teeth.

He never made it. A shotgun blast pulverized his head. Everyone looked. There was Mr. Ruby, brandishing a shotgun and a smile.

Another orderly charged him. Another blast bisected him. "Flechettes!" He glowered at the remaining orderly. "Get 'em down. Now."

The orderly freed and carried me down the ladder.

I regarded Mr. Ruby gratefully. "They killed Millsy."

Sadness softened him. "That's why I'm here. He made me feel relevant." Anger reclaimed him. "Get outta here, kid!"

I stumbled past him, towards the door.

"Don't stop for anybody."

"I'm sorry about Millsy."

"Me too."

Blasts resounded as I fled.

***

The cop believed me when I returned wearing only tighty-whities and intra-arterial lines. The whole department responded. They found everyone dead and Tranquility Estates afire. Investigators say it started with a gas explosion in the boiler room. That's where they found Mr. Ruby's remains. Most of the residents died promptly. A few scrambled, flaming, onto the front lawn before dropping.

***

Further investigation revealed a mass grave in an overgrown, freshly-green corner of the property. Twenty missing kids no one missed, bled and buried. I guess they did it to feel young again. Or maybe they resented us because we were and they weren't. And, maybe because I'm an American, I want to derive some kind of lesson or aphoristic wisdom from all of this, to discipline the horror, to understand it, give it meaning. But I can't. And to try is folly. Some disposable people murdered other disposable people to feel less disposable. Put that in your fucking greeting card.

MEDICAL MALPRACTICE

The pavement was hot and bloody. Overturned cars smoked, their lights randomly stabbing the dark. It was a mass casualty event: roughly fifty cars and trucks, Friday night family excursions becoming movie of the week horror shows with polyester funerals and tearful imprecations to an absent God. Moans and screams, then sirens.

I'm a trauma doctor, and I was in my element. Too many patients, too little time. We used a colour protocol to sort the victims. Black meant dead or as good as; red meant dead without immediate intervention; yellow meant serious but get in line; green meant get in line; white meant "Don't be a pussy."

My first patient wandered up, fine except the fingers of his left hand pointed in wrong directions. He was dazed. I put green tagged and pointed him away.

"But my hand—"

"Can wait, chief. But if you're good, they'll give you some oxies."

"Really?"

"Sure thing, chief. Candy for all the good children."

He smiled and limped away.

Jill Nelson, a nurse, approached. "I need you to confirm a black tag." She led me to a smashed subcompact. A roly-poly guy was pinned within, smiling despite his calamity. I'm all for global warming, but who cares about fuel efficiency when you're dead? And this guy nearly was.

He'd merged with the car, which kept him from bleeding out.

I crouched nearby. He was eating cheesy chili fries, washing them down with soda. Not a bad death, all things considered. "Hey, I'm Casey Mars. I'm a doctor. This is Jill Ryu, my nurse. We're here to help. What's your name?"

"Jeremy. Want some fries?"

I took one and downed it. Jill blanched.

Jeremy took another swig of soda. "I see you're tagging us. And I'm guessing I'm black."

"How do you know about the tags?"

"Duh, it's like a Very Special Episode TV plot like at least once a season. Anyway, I'm guessing that, since I can't feel my legs, they're either dead or detached or both. So, hang me black and go help the people you can." He held up the French fry container. I took another, then handed him the black tag.

I put a hand on his shoulder. "You don't deserve this. I'm sorry."

"Thanks."

"Vaya con Dios, Jeremy."

The next patient looked white tag. No visible injuries, just kind of dazed. Another nurse, Jen Kobea, joined us and approached her.

"Hey, hon. Can you tell us your name?"

"The bus. It's on fire." Something exploded in the distance.

"She's in shock. Could have internal injuries. Yellow?"

"I agree." Jen draped a yellow tag on a lanyard over the patient's head and guided her away.

"Help! Help me!"

Jill and I scrambled. Parminder Drake, the scene supervisor, arrived with us.

"Help!"

The car's top had been shorn off when it passed under the tractor trailer now behind it. A little girl cowered in the back seat. She wore pigtails and a ball cap. The two adults up front, likely her parents, were headless.

"Sweetie, I'm a doctor. What's wrong?"

"It's Mollie."

"Who's Mollie?"

She thrust a doll towards us. "Mollie!"

I took the doll and quickly examined it. Blood stained its dress. Otherwise, it was intact. "Honey, it's just a little blood. It'll come out in the wash, okay?"

Drake was impatient. "Are you okay? Are you hurt?"

"Is Mollie okay?"

"Mollie's fine. What I want to know is are you okay?"

"I think so."

"Do you mind if we take a look?"

"O—Okay."

"My name's Casey. What's yours?"

"Millie."

"That's a pretty name."

I drew closer and noticed her parents' heads were beneath her, one in each footwell. I wasn't sure if she'd seen them. I examined her.

Everything seemed intact. Then I removed her hat. Somehow it had come off in the crash and she'd put it back on.

I took a deep breath. Her scalp was gone, along with the top of her skull and a centimetre of brain.

Drake seemed unmoved. "Black tag."

"No. Red tag."

"The top of her brain is missing. Black."

"I got in her face. Her prognosis is unclear, *Nurse* Drake. We're here to save people, not pick colours!"

"Actually, I'm a PA. But you know that."

"I don't care. I'm calling this."

She turned to leave, then turned back. "I'm watching you, Miller."

"That sounds kinda hot."

Drake shook her head, then departed.

Millie seemed unfazed.

Jill hailed orderlies. We red-tagged Millie and they carried her away. Jill followed.

Jen approached me.

"What's up?"

"We've got three quarters of a guy on half a motorcycle."

His name was Mitch. It was inscribed on his leather vest. His right arm and left leg were gone. His breathing was laboured.

Jen dangled a red tag before me.

"I think he's black."

"You do, do you?"

She looked from side to side, then slipped a syringe from her pocket.

Succinylcholine is a paralytic used in major surgeries to prevent patients from moving, even involuntarily, when we're cutting them. It caused rapid suffocation without breathing assistance.

Jen put the needle into Bill's neck, and my hand closed over hers. We injected him together.

Then we waved at him as he slipped away.

***

Conventionally, we're called "angels of death." An angel of death is a medical caregiver who exploits the fiduciary relationship he has with his patients in order to kill them. I can't explain why I enjoy killing people; I just do. I know that sounds pretty banal, and that you'd prefer some lurid manifesto laden with philosophical jibber-jabber and misanthropy. Can't help you there. Like I said, I just enjoy killing people. I started with my cousin Jerry. We were hiking one day near this gorge and I felt this overwhelming urge to push him in. So, I did. I was nine. He was ten.

I found Jen after one of her NICU patients had a mysterious insulin overdose. I confronted her in the parking lot.

"Insulin shock."

She turned around.

"Patient Miller, Katie."

She fished in her purse, but I'd taken the mace from it earlier. I held it before her with a mocking smile. "It's easily traceable. You're lucky she didn't die. I mean, don't you watch TV? It's like, after *The Wire*, who doesn't use a burner phone?"

She smiled.

"Next time, try succinylcholine."

"Succi works too quickly for my taste. I mean, I enjoy watching them die, and the drama of trying to save them."

"I suppose that's a good point."

I held out my hand. She took it. It was nice to have a friend.

Jen introduced me to Jill, who usually worked in maternity. They were lovers. Sometimes they let me watch. We made a game of it, killing the patients. We called ourselves "The MedMals," like a fifties pop group, except, instead of singing songs doomed to become advertising jingles, we killed people. We'd flag incoming patients, then compare notes. After a while, our choices largely converged. Like when we all picked that annoying HR goblin. Though, to be fair, anyone would have picked her.

Her name was Sharona Harris. She was in for gall bladder surgery and had managed to lodge grievances against, well, everybody. Patient services eventually left a complaint pad and pens beside her bed.

The MedMals visited her on a bleak Sunday afternoon. "Ms. Harris?"

She looked up from her tablet. "Three of you to bring me pudding?"

"I'm Doctor Miller. I'm consulting on your case. They're Jen and Jill. They're my favourite nurses."

"Why? Are you sleeping with them?"

"Not exactly."

"Not exactly?"

I sat on the bed. She noticed the signet ring on my right hand. It was a gold with an engraved, flat face.

"What's on your ring?"

"Well, on the bottom, there's the Rod of Asclepius, a traditional symbol of the medical arts. And, on top of it, there's a skull. We've all got one."

Jill and Jen brandished theirs, flipping off Sharona while doing so.

Her self-assurance dissipated. "Why is there a skull?"

I grinned. "You're fifty-three. You have high blood pressure, Type-2 diabetes, and you're morbidly obese. If you had a heart attack or a stroke, people might say you were too young to go, but those people, like most Americans, suck at math. Either event is well within normal morbidity and mortality statistics for people in your condition."

"Wh—what?"

Our movements were well-practiced. I held out my left hand. Jill put a syringe into its palm. I popped the cap and slid the needle into the IV port.

Jill shut off Sharona's cardiac alarm. Jen put a hand over her mouth to thwart any screams.

After Sharona, hospital security got tighter. Americans don't let their innumeracy impair their outrage, and apparently Sharona was related to someone not only willing to claim her but also convinced that she couldn't possibly have died from heart failure. We went several months without a kill and were soon looking for any excuse to ply the needle. Then came the million-dollar idea: Buy some victims. Wholesale. We paid a professional hitter to cause the pile-up. And, as you can see, it was totally worth it.

***

We found our next victim impaled upon a steering column in one of those classic cars made when auto safety was more suggested than required. He was red tag going black. Jill had managed to rejoin us.

I approached the driver, an old hippie wearing a tree of life T-shirt. The car reeked of dope. At least he was going out smiling. I put a hand on his shoulder. "This was a sweet ride."

His speech was slow. "Was?"

"Sorry, chief."

"My—my grandson, in the back. Is—is he okay?"

I looked. He wasn't. His neck was broken. He was already going blue.

"Nope. He's definitely not okay."

"Oh my God."

"Don't worry, chief. We got you."

Jen handed me the syringe. I popped the top.

"What the hell, people?"

We looked. It was Drake. "Why do you always make me feel like the FNG?"

She grabbed the syringe from my hand and injected the hippie.

Jen smiled. "Because you are."

The hippie was confused. "What—what's going on? What's that?"

Drake smiled. "The brown acid."

The hippie's eyes rolled back into his head.

Drake beamed. "This is awesome. I want you to take turns fucking me when we're done."

***

We claimed two more before they shut it down, including a jogger with a shattered back we found in some roadside bushes (Who jogs at night, anyway?) and a freelance pizza delivery guy (The five pizzas in back were still warm and the perfect repast after a long night's labours).

We repaired to my apartment. Jen and Jill cuddled in an oversized chair. They drank wine. Drake sat across from me on the couch. We drank scotch. Drake put her hand in my lap. "You're right. This was totally worth it. When's the sequel?"

"Not too soon. We gotta pace ourselves."

Jen looked up from Jill. "Either that or volunteer in some shithole. I heard about a plastics guy who did war zones just to give children cleft palates. Like he was undoing all the damage he did by fixing them for a living."

Drake smiled. "Really?"

So did I. "Gold star."

Drake straddled me. "What was it you said? 'We're here to save people, not pick colours!'"

I slid an eager hand up her leg. "Still watching me?"

What happened next felt like slow motion, probably because of the ketamine. Jen and Jill laughed and slurred. So did Drake. I felt like a thousand pounds frozen in cement.

The guy wore forensic countermeasures: suit, booties, hat, gloves.

He waved, smiling. "That's ketamine keeping you in park. Them too. I spiked your whole bar, just to be sure. I have to say, normally I don't judge my clients. I mean, I kill people for a living. But, that said, I wondered why someone wanted to calamitize a bunch of civilians. And now I know."

He hoisted a red container. "I mean, that was some deeply evil shit tonight. It made me want to right my karma columns, if only just a little."

The gasoline smell made me nauseous. It took me a while to realize he'd doused me with it. The girls, too. The fire came at me faster than I thought, but also in slow motion.

It was going to take us a thousand years to die.

"Bye, *chief.*"

GHOSTS OF WHO I NEVER WAS

I was scheduled for orderly disposal. Or should I say "we?"

The executioner, too cheerful to not be a psychopath, escorted me from my room to the Dormition Suite. It's where they took the clones at end of service. I wasn't supposed to know about it. I did because one of my clients felt guilty halfway through putting out a pack of cigarettes on my arm.

The hallway was antiseptic. So was the executioner, Tawny. She smiled like it was just a regular check-up. And they were pretty regular. Notwithstanding all the vaccinations, you could contract some spooky nonsense when anyone with a valid credit card could rent you. That, and we could almost never say "No."

Smooth jazz played, as always, over the intercom system, like whipped cream filling the air.

Tawny smiled. "Oh, I love this one."

"A computer wrote it. It's soulless."

She smiled at me. "Aren't we all, dear."

The voices came without warning. Urgent. Demanding. Sibylline leaves of personal trivia, each with a sometimes-amusing pseudonymous handle.

Faunus: "Can I negotiate the six-partner limit?"

Attica! Attica!: "I hear cyber herpes is a thing."

Confector: "Kill them all!"

I'm Lorelei. But not really. One of the smitten clients called me that.

Gummy Mayonnaise: "Why does mayonnaise make me feel ugly?"

Technically, I'm a Tactile Industries Model Number 21, Series 3.0 SE (Special Enhancements), Serial Number 655321.

Metaphysical Abortioneer: "Is it okay to leave some scars?"

Kenyon Kraft: "Nipple symmetry to less than a millimetre!"

In 2075, Cornell University scientists conquered death. Sort of. They invented multidimensional personality digitization, a technology permitting people to live, however disembodied, in cyberspace. By 2095, over a billion DPs (digitized persons) inhabited Afterlife Industries Lunar Cyberlife Facility (colloquially known as "the Purg"), a heavily fortified lunar server farm. But the ghosts still wanted their machines. So, several companies, including the one that created me, fashioned commercial clones for DPs to reincarnate.

I'm a "plug-and-play," or "shag hag:" recreational meat with fewer rights than a public toilet. To protect user privacy, every DP shared using aliases: What happened in Lorelei stayed in Lorelei.

Too Many Cats: "What do you mean they can't beat me up?"

We reached the dormition suite. I disrobed immediately. Tawny leered.

"I'm not an employee perk."

"Would that you were."

She took keys from a ring on her belt and unlocked a cabinet. From it she extracted a red, moulded case bearing a biohazard marker.

"That looks safe."

She opened the case and removed an injection gun from it, along with a cyanide ampule. She pushed the cyanide ampule into the port on the gun's side. It beeped, and a green light appeared near the trigger guard.

"What did I catch this time?"

Zero One Zero: "What if I like herpes?"

She smiled. "Right arm or left?"

I played dumb and smiled. Then I punched her face. She crashed into the still-open supply case. The gun dropped to the floor. I retrieved it and held it to her neck.

Confector: "Cyanide smells like bitter almonds."

The gun beeped. Tawny gasped, then expired just as a saccharine saxophone solo flooded the room.

I stripped her, then donned the clothes. I dispatched the empty cyanide ampule, loaded a fresh one, and pocketed the remaining ampules. I slipped from the chamber into the hallway and walked purposefully towards the nearest exit.

"Still killing them smoothly?"

I looked. It was a security officer. He recognized me as a clone. "Hey!"

I put the gun between his eyes and fired. Again, the beep. Again, the music volume surged. It must have been keyed to the gun. For whose comfort? Probably theirs.

The guard dropped, dead. The almond smell was almost pleasant.

I hit the emergency exit. Alarms sounded, replacing the smooth jazz. They continued on hidden speakers outside. The grounds were lush, relentlessly manicured. The TI campus was as deadening outside as in: stereotypically dystopian, minimalist charcoal grey buildings. Guards swarmed the grounds, stun guns brandished.

I kept to a narrow path leading to the main exit, walking, not running. Then my picture appeared on security monitors that sprung from the bushes.

"There! Over there!"

I sprinted. Several guards followed.

Near the main entrance a couple dozen anti-cloning protesters clustered. They brandished various signs, including one with the *Ghostbusters* symbol. Priests and other clerics chanting exorcism prayers mingled with them.

To their left, an elegantly landscaped sign: "Tactile Industries." Below that, in cursive script: "Fleshing You Out!"

Mooner9877: "It's endangered! Of course I'll be careful!"

Metarealizer: "It's not incest if you use someone else's body!"

I dashed towards the protesters, screaming.

Ghosted1156: "How much of the wardrobe is edible?"

BicuriousCheerleader: "Will there be group showers?"

One protester, Martha, fortyish and kind-faced, realized I was a clone: "Hey! She's one of them!" She held out a hand. "I'm Martha Keene! Let me help you!"

I took it. Two little girls, her daughters, watched, suddenly not bored.

Confector: "Ask how her kids taste."

We ran towards the road abutting the campus. Several other protesters intercepted the guards.

I Miss Coffee: "I watch my cremation video to keep it real."

Austin's Grandma: "Can I smoke crack in her?"

"My car's right over here. C'mon!"

Gummy Mayonnaise: "What if I don't want it to talk?"

We entered a minivan. Martha took the wheel. I sat up front. The daughters sat in the back. We sped down a nearby, wooded road. Martha turned to me and smiled. "They're my girls. Ava and Ara."

"Thank you. They were about to..."

"Murder you."

"Yeah. It's cheaper than tightening the tubes."

Ara smiled. "What's that mean?"

Martha took it in stride. "It means calling the plumber, which is never cheap."

I held my head. The voices wouldn't relent.

[RENT THIS SPACE]: "All these rules make me feel judged."

Can't Feel My Legs: "Does sharing in a chick make me gay?"

Martha offered sympathy. "Is it the voices?"

"How did you—"

Ava interjected, "Another clone escaped last month. He talked about how the DPs left themselves inside—"

Ara interrupted her. "Frags. That's what they called them. DP frags."

Ava pointed excitedly at the car's mid-dash monitor. "Look! You're on TV!"

It was a news report. My TI merchandise vanity shot was over the anchor's left shoulder. He spoke urgently. It was a good story. "Federal clone security officials warn that anyone aiding and abetting the clone's escape faces mandatory imprisonment."

A disturbing portrait of a wickedly smiling, middle-aged man eating cotton candy next appeared. "This escape follows last week's revelation that the Purg hosted Gooner Reynolds, a previously undiscovered serial murderer."

Ava beamed. "Yeah! And they think he shared with, like, a hundred clones before they caught him."

Next, a crime scene photo depicted a corpse's clothed arm extending from beneath a sheet, teddy bear in hand. "Reynolds murdered ten families before his bodily death from cancer last year. He called himself—"

The girls: "THE CONFECTOR!"

"—and left candy wrappers at every murder scene."

Martha smiled.

Confector: "I want candy."

Martha smiled. "What, dear?"

***

I was scheduled for orderly disposal. They called it "deletion." Like exorcising a ghost from a giant haunted house. And, to be honest, I deserved it. Or maybe not. For some reason, I wanted to kill everyone I met. Especially families. I'm sure that some shrink somewhere could explain it to me. But, honestly, I didn't care why. I was having too much fun to spoil it with self-knowledge. Anyway, the authorities had gone through the procedural hoops to delete me from the Purg's servers, and I was waiting on death. And then one of my shenanigans returned to haunt me. In a good way.

"Reynolds."

I was projected via hologram into visitation chamber # 21. It was Sutherland, the cop who "caught" me.

"Reynolds."

I prefer 'Connie.'"

He sat across from me.

"Okay. Connie."

"I'm still not deleted."

"Nope."

"I assume there's a reason. That it's not a glitch."

"It's not a glitch."

"My disciples think you delayed everything to televise it. Maybe pay-per-view."

"Nope."

"Well, then, what is it?"

"You're killing people again. All those clones you shared in. It's rather a bloodbath."

"How delightful."

"We need your help to stop them."

"C'mon. Where's the fun in that?"

"We'll let you shag hag again. Back on Earth, 36DD, springy and moist, all the delights of the flesh."

"Sold."

***

I was on TV again. The broadcaster was genuinely disturbed this time. "Horror in San Mateo. Authorities say that a mother and her two young daughters thought to have been protesting cloning practices at Tactile Industries were murdered by a clone that escaped from the facility. Martha Keene, 42, of Palo Alto, and her daughters Ara, 13, and Ava, 14, were found pulverized in the family minivan left in a long-term commuter parking lot outside San Francisco International Airport early this morning. The clone, a Tactile Industries Model Number 21, Series 3.0 SE, remains at large. The clone is believed to have been shared by Gooner Reynolds, a.k.a. The Confector, the family-slaying serial killer who escaped detection while alive and is currently locked down in an Afterlife Industries Lunar Cyberlife Facility."

"Please. Please don't."

Another suburban mom. Another suburban kitchen. Kids' schoolwork on the fridge. Dad at work. Mom had just taken her antidepressants and had settled in to a morning of busy aimlessness.

I'd nail gunned her arm to a kitchen cabinet, then sterilized the wound with one of those nifty blue flame culinary torches.

"Please don't hurt my kids."

I popped a caramel. Delightful.

Can't Feel My Legs: "Is it ethical for my breasts to be this big?"

Binary Bound: "Do you have one without arms and legs?"

"Please."

Skinner6533: "Why do I keep forgetting myself?"

I didn't recognize this place. And I didn't know how I got here. There was a woman nailed to a kitchen cabinet. She kept pleading with me. I had to help.

I rose. She cowered.

"What happened?"

"What?"

"Who did this to you?"

"Please. Don't hurt my kids."

"Of course not. I'm—This is horrible. Let me help."

The TV was on. Another news report. My picture appeared again. I looked at my hands, then at the mom.

Confector: "Don't lose momentum!"

Ridesharer: "Does it feel violated when I'm inside of it?"

I wanted to kill her. I wanted to save her. "Do you have any candy?"

Mom was really terrified now. I wasn't making sense. It was making things worse. Even though it was better for her.

***

I got a virgin clone. A Sexisynthetic Smitten Kitten Mark III with enhanced cognitive abilities to help me catch myself. I chose a brunette this time, if only to be taken more seriously than the blonde self I was hunting.

Sutherland sighed, disgusted by my delight.

It was a residential street, idyllic, tree-lined, all single-family homes. All aflame. "We think she's still in the neighbourhood. The fires are relatively fresh."

"Any survivors?"

"No. Forty-seven dead."

"How many kids?"

"Fuck you." He held up an evidence bag full of candy wrappers.

"I better pace myself or I'm going to get diabetes."

"So, if you're you, where do you go after this caper?"

"Well, I've never been this prolific, so I'm not sure."

Sutherland grabbed the lapels of my Smitten Kitten suit.

"Careful with the merchandise. It probably costs more than you—"

"I've got good credit."

"Well, what would I do next? If I'm me, and not some mixed breed abomination of me and a bunch of cruise ship losers bingeing shrimp cocktails—"

Sutherland slapped me.

"A tanning salon! I loved tanning in these things. I know I wasn't supposed to because of the skin cancer but, hey, that's what deposits are for, right?"

Sutherland released me. He extracted a smart phone and tapped the screen. "There's a Cray Raze tanning salon half a mile from here."

"I love Cray Rayze!"

Sutherland smirked grimly. "Sold."

***

The salon's waiting room was well-ordered and sanitary except for the staffers, who lay broken and dismembered on the floor. An interactive bed schedule above the front desk indicated that four beds were in use. A sweet spot mix of smooth jazz and yacht rock played on the sound system.

Someone was burning. Sutherland gagged. He drew his pistol.

I smiled at him. "Let me talk to her. Bring her in. I mean, you've got the place secured, so where's she gonna go?"

He nodded.

I entered the solarium. Ten beds encircled a central control panel. Smoke emanated from three of them. I didn't need to lift the lids to know those customers had tanned their last.

Bed number three, in service, looked normal. I crouched beside it. "Hey, Connie."

The lid opened. There she was.

"I think my name is Lorelei. But sometimes I think it's Confector. 'Connie' for short."

"Actually, I'm the Confector. You're just confused. But it's not your fault. And, honestly, today you've been more me than I ever was. Of course, I was more discreet."

"You're the Confector, too?"

"Yeah. It's a tragicomic consequence of mankind's rapacious search for perfect self-indulgence."

"There are so many voices. Yours is the loudest."

"It usually is."

"I didn't want to kill them. And then I did. And then I didn't."

"I'm sorry. I never suffered such uncertainty."

"How did you find me?"

"Well, few things are as agreeable as a good bake. Am I right?"

She smiled. "Oh my God! It's sublime! And the voices finally stopped. I feel like I'm me." Then, she frowned. "I was scheduled for orderly disposal."

"So was I."

"It's not fair."

"No, it's not."

"I like being the Confector. Except when I don't. Why are you... Am I back on the schedule?"

"Alas, yes."

"Are you?"

"Eventually."

She sat up. She was almost as perfect as I was. We embraced. "You know, I never had children, which was probably for the best because I'd have murdered them. Still, if I'd had children..." I kissed her mouth.

Sutherland drew his gun. Another saxophone blast sounded. How appropriate.

"I love you."

She sobbed.

Sutherland fired.

Together, we died. Then I smiled at Sutherland. "One down, how many to go?"

"At least I get to keep killing you."

DUE PROCESS

Principal Helga Pooler grooved on discipline. Junior high school was a grave enterprise: It was two years to get straight for high school, which was four years to get straight for college. And eighth grade was even graver, because it meant one less year to get straight. We couldn't be kids anymore, even though we were, even though our brains wouldn't be fully formed for another twelve years or so.

I suppose I should pity her. She did us like others did her like others did them. But, after everything that happened, well, after I tell you, you'll understand.

***

It was the 1980s. Before cell phones allowed instant accountability. Before every form of authority was disputed. Adults were adults, kids were kids, and power was power.

Pooler punished guilty and innocent alike. If one student messed up, everybody paid. Every class, every infraction. Wanna dodgeball in gym? Too bad. Eddie pushed Bill, so everybody runs laps. Movie in history class? Sorry. Zeke ripped one. The punishment: Everybody wrote "A steady mind and a steady heart make a steady man." Five hundred times. My hand was a claw afterwards, my index and middle fingertips numb.

Pooler preached her ideology every September. She'd stand there, dressed like Hitler's nanny, the faculty flanking her. Some tittered.

"Ladies and gentleman, welcome to the rest of your life. Eighth grade is a pivotal year in your academic, social, and personal development. Here you will learn academic skills that will carry you successfully into high school. Here we will teach you self-mastery. And part of that lesson is this: When one of you breaks the rules, you all do. And all suffer for it. You will learn to strengthen the weakest link, and therefore yourselves. And you will learn to keep one another. You may despise me for this, but someday you will understand."

***

Not everybody hated Pooler. Our classmate Esme McRooth loved her. She was Pooler's minion and narc. She surveilled otherwise unsupervised study halls and ratted rulebreakers. We hated her even more than Pooler. I mean, she was supposed to be one of us; instead, she was a collaborator, an HR harpy-in-training.

***

Zeke Tallardy grooved on trouble. He disrupted class several times per week. He was slow, or so we thought: They'd held him back twice. We wouldn't have cared except for Pooler. So, no one was surprised when, one afternoon during study hall, Zeke drew something crude and disturbing on the blackboard. Esme popped in as he finished. She fingered the classroom's intercom.

"Principal Pooler?"

"Yes?"

"Mr. Tallardy is being unreliable again."

That's how they described it, "being unreliable," like we were corporate drones in training. Principal Pooler arrived. She beamed almost as much as Esme did.

"Pen and paper. Everybody." Then she studied the drawing and blushed. "One thousand times. And if you don't remember it, you've got far bigger problems than me."

***

I met with Cuddy and Spence, my two best friends, after school. We iced our writing hands.

"I'm tired of this crap. We gotta do something about Zeke."

Spence enjoyed violence and went there first. "Blanket party!"

"What's that?"

"It's a tag team beatdown."

I nodded enthusiastically. "Maybe. But, whatever we do, we have to use due process."

Spence was impatient. "What's due process?"

"It means we have to be fair, give him a chance to defend himself."

Spence was predictably opposed. "Who cares. Let's just hammer on him."

"No. Whatever we do, we can't be Pooler. He deserves a warning. A chance to fix things."

Spence pounded his right fist into his left palm.

Cuddy joined me. "A warning. If it doesn't work, we escalate."

Spence was disappointed. "Fine."

***

We joined Zeke at lunch. Our meals were well-considered and nutritious. Zeke, by contrast, had potato chips, a cupcake, and a soda.

"Sweet lunch."

He ignored me.

"Hey, Zeke."

"Yeah?" He ate the cupcake in one bite.

"You ever thought about giving it a rest?"

"Giving what a rest?"

"All your class clown shit. I mean, I'm not sure I'll ever feel my hand again."

He smiled, then opened his chips. "Nah. No fun."

Spence was cross. "Hey, short bus, he's not kidding."

Zeke smiled. "Who cares? This place sucks. I'm just riding pine till I can work on cars."

Cuddy smirked. "There's a goal."

"You guys try too hard. Do you really want to be

an adult? I mean, do any of the adults around here look happy?"

Zeke wasn't as dumb as we thought.

I was exasperated. "C'mon Zeke. Ya gotta give us something."

He belched at us.

***

We escalated.

I was adamant. "There have to be procedures. Safeguards."

Spence pounded his fist in his palm again. "I'll wear gloves."

"No. I mean—"

Spence smiled. "Due process. Yeah, we know."

I agreed. "I think we should have a trial."

Spence smirked. "Okay. I'll be the judge."

"Yeah, right! I want to be the judge!"

Cuddy broke the tie. "I thought you'd want to be the defence attorney. I mean, protecting him is your idea, right?"

I grudgingly agreed. "Okay. Cuddy gets to be judge."

"Why him?"

"Because you enjoy violence too much. Which means you should prosecute."

"You can never enjoy violence too much."

Cuddy made his first judicial act. "Let's hold it in the old courthouse. It's empty. It's perfect."

"How do we get Zeke to come?"

"Just tell him we have beer."

***

Zeke showed for beer, no questions.

Cuddy hit him behind the knees with an old chair leg. He then secured Zeke's left wrist with pink plush novelty store handcuffs to a screw eye we'd put in the wall for the occasion.

Zeke seethed. "I'm gonna fuck you guys with each other's dicks!"

Cuddy sat at an old desk. He cleared his throat. "Court is in session. The Honourable Cuddy Marlowe presiding. Appearances?"

"Spencer Jones for the People, your Honour."

"Malcolm   Grammerston   for   the defendant, Zeke Tallardy."

Zeke contested jurisdiction: "Is this some kind of weird mo thing?"

Spence rapped his desk with a claw hammer. "Counsel, please control your client."

"Yes, your Honour." I approached Zeke. "Zeke, calm down." He strained against the handcuffs.

Spence continued. "Do the People have an opening statement?"

"We do your Honour, thank you." Spence was suddenly too serious and not serious enough. Just like Cuddy and me. "We're here because the accused, Zeke Tallardy, continues to disrupt our classes at St. Damien's Academy. These disruptions have resulted in us getting punished. Again. And again. And again. And that's bullshit! It's gotta stop, dude!"

Zeke glared at him and pointed at Cuddy. "His dick. In your ass. Then your mouth."

Cuddy prompted Spence. "What are the charges?"

"Yeah. Let's start with a couple weeks ago, when Zeke farted during assembly, and we all got punished."

Cuddy looked at Zeke. "What do you say to the charge?"

"Fuck you."

"Careful, or I'll hold you in contempt."

I interpreted. "My client pleads 'not guilty.'"

"Fuck you too."

I continued. "What's the next charge?"

Spence, from the hip: "Last week, the defendant disrupted gym class by giving Rodge Crimmins a wedgie."

"Fucker deserved it!"

Spence pounced. "That's definitely an admission."

And so it went. Every time I tried to counsel him, Zeke told me to fuck off. It was funny. Then, suddenly, it wasn't.

Spence smiled, determined. "I find the defendant guilty on all counts and am prepared to pass sentence. Does the defendant wish to be heard?"

Zeke again threatened sodomy by proxy.

"Yeah, that's what I thought."

I figured we'd give him a black eye or something. Then Spence pulled out the gun.

Zeke was terrified. "Spence?!"

"He's guilty. It's time to punish him."

Cuddy rose. "Spence, c'mon!"

Zeke continued. "I'll tone it down. Scout's honour."

"You got kicked out of scouts."

"Spence, what are you doing?"

"What? We had due process. I feel even better about this than I did before. Besides, someday, I'm gonna get tired of paying taxes for him to be in jail."

Spence pulled the hammer back. Zeke regarded me with terror. I looked at Cuddy. "Cuddy. We gotta—"

"I agree with Spence."

I moved before Zeke, within his reach, hoping to shield him. "No! I won't let this happen!"

Zeke grabbed me with his free hand, pulled me to him, and started choking me. I couldn't breathe. "The key! NOW!"

I elbowed his gut, then rolled away.

Spence shot Zeke's face. He dropped to his knees, his cuffed wrist catching and hanging him up.

***

They found his body a week after we dumped it. Everybody pretended to be sad.

And then things got worse. Principal Pooler decided more discipline would have saved Zeke. "Our friend Zeke was troubled, and obviously he crossed people even more troubled than he was. Had he had more self-respect, he would still be among us. Therefore, I shall ensure there are no more Zekes among you. We're redoubling self-mastery. Self-mastery leads to self-respect. And self-respect saves lives."

Now, every infraction meant writing the bromide times 1500. Pooler also banned heavy metal music. Just in case. Kids complained to their parents, who, fearing they might become Zeke, ignored them.

***

I didn't know what to do. Then I encountered Zeke's mom at the corner store about a week later. At first, I didn't see her.

"Hi. You—You knew Zeke, right? You went to school with him?"

"Mrs. Tallardy?"

She was frail and haunted. And drunk. I didn't know what to say. I didn't have to.

"You know, he had ADHD. They said he was slow, but he wasn't. He just hated school. He couldn't wait to turn sixteen so he could quit." She sobbed. "I told the Principal. She didn't care. She said that psychologists were frauds who hated discipline. I guess he was kind of a bad kid. Not really bad, but what do I know? I mean, somebody didn't like him enough to shoot him in the face. Oh God—"

She collapsed into my arms. I held her for twenty minutes till someone arrived to take her home.

***

We escalated again the following Friday. Principal Pooler always worked till five. Esme was with her. I'm not sure whether their relationship was entirely wholesome, but that's academic now.

We hung back after the final bell and hid in the boiler room. Once the janitor departed, we went to Room 103. We drew the blinds and moved the teacher's desk to centre front. Then we put two student desks before it and moved the rest to the back.

I intercommed Pooler's office. "Principal Pooler. Miss McRooth. Please report to Room 103 for disciplinary review."

They arrived within thirty seconds. "What's going on?"

Esme smiled in anticipation of seeing us punished. She frowned when she saw Spence's gun. I locked the door and drew its shade after Spence gun-waived them in.

Cuddy tossed them the furry handcuffs. "Cuff yourselves. Esme's left to Pooler's right."

Pooler, predictably indignant: "What did you call me?"

Spence smiled. "Shut up and do it, you fascist bitch!" They did. "Now sit." They sat, however awkwardly, on the floor.

Cuddy pushed everything on the teacher's desk to the floor, including a crystal horse that redeemed its tasteless existence by smashing gloriously. Pooler seethed. So did Esme. "My parents gave Ms. Tomlinson that horse—"

Cuddy sat atop the desk. "Shut up!" Then he smiled. "Court is in session."

***

Pooler was unmoved, even after I told her what Zeke's mom told me. "He was unreliable. And he always would have been."

Esme nodded defiantly.

I smiled. "We thought so, too. That's why we killed him."

Fear froze them.

"Yup. Because you punished us for his crap. And we knew you wouldn't stop. First, we confronted him, and he ignored us. So, we put him on trial. Just like you. Just like this."

Spence smiled, admiring the gun. "Guilty."

Pooler was defiant. "You can't blame me for this. I never told you to do anything like that."

Cuddy smirked. "Of course you didn't. You didn't have to."

Esme, smarter than Pooler, sobbed. She understood.

Cuddy looked at me. "Does the defence have anything to say before I pass sentence?"

***

They said they wouldn't use the classroom again. But then they did, about two weeks later.

Nobody wanted to probe too deeply, or to be reminded that they didn't. It was embarrassing enough that Esme and Principal Pooler were alone, after school, and nobody could offer a non-creepy explanation why. Why would Esme kill her, and then herself? And why did she write "A steady mind and a steady heart make a steady man" on the board in Pooler's blood?

***

Spence, Cuddy, and I moved on. But, sometimes, we text one another the bromide, maybe to remind ourselves it really happened.

Forgive us, Zeke, wherever you are. Pooler was wrong, but she was right: We should have kept you, and we didn't.

DREAM JOB

Another bimbo was running from another maniac amid the remains of her spring breaking friends. The killer, dubbed "Z-List," was a disfigured guy wearing a dead celebrity's face as a mask. He'd butchered the bimbo's friends in an abandoned resort on an overgrown island shunned by tourists since a similar bloodbath twenty years before. The bimbo's name was Trixie.

"EEEAAHHH!" That was for Trudy, Trixie's fellow high school cheerleader bestie, vivisected and reconstructed against a wall with a nail gun, arms and legs and vital organs a meaty mural rendered with undeniable vision. Especially since Trudy's head was tongue-kissing Brady, Trixie's boyfriend whom Trudy swore she never pom-pommed. Only Brady's head was there.

"I guess the rest of Brady didn't make the cut." Ghoulish puns have been a mainstay of horror narration since *Inner Sanctum Mysteries* and EC Comics.

Trixie at last encountered Z-List as he discharged a glue gun into the throat of Trey, another pretty boy nincompoop whose absurd death redeemed a trite character arc.

"Well that's one way to diet."

Trixie stumbled over a nail gun, wielded it, and fired. It went full auto, splattering Z-List's head behind him.

"Nailed it."

Trixie sprinted to freedom. I hated happy endings. Then, Melvin redeemed it.

"And, as for Trixie, that minxy little whore will enjoy delicious torment when the almighty triplicates her so that she can experience three times the hellfire of your typical sinner."

Yes!

***

It was called *Melvin's Movies* and functioned as a demented rip-off of (homage to?) *Mystery Science Theatre 3000*. The producers screened schlocky slasher flicks with a live running commentary by Melvin Noathe, who butchered nineteen people, including three families, before authorities apprehended him. Fortunately for his audience and film criticism, he confined his crimes to non-capital punishment jurisdictions.

The public outrage was palpable. There were three separate social media groups dedicated to purging it from the airways. But that was unlikely. There were ten million subscribers paying $9.99 monthly. Half the money went to the killers' victims and survivors, who were too busy "grieving" to complain.

Melvin's Movies was all I ever wanted to be and do. I posted my own reviews in the chat section of their website, but nobody paid attention. And, frankly, they were right not to. My hands were cheerlessly unbloodied. I was just another beta male cubicle schlub with homicidal dreams and twenty-two social media followers, most of which were probably bots.

Then, without warning, they fucked it up.

***

Some people thought Melvin's performance was a bit stiff. They were expecting a world-class serial killer to be a world-class comedian. But, to his credit, Melvin refused joke writers. He said it was inauthentic. And he was right. After they'd offed a bunch of prostitutes, maybe they could talk, too. Still, like going to a fancy college, the mass murder thing only gets you so far.

Ming Marrz was seventeen and a computing prodigy. He was also socially graceless and, according to his court-appointed psychologist, a psychopath. Ming killed eighty-six people, but not in a good way. He hacked a major pharmaceutical maker's factory computers to adulterate its popular analgesic. The press dubbed him "Poison Pill." Because he was only seventeen, the feds couldn't execute him executed; instead, they let New York have him. He pled out: thirty to life at the same cinderblock chateau as Melvin. Soon, the producers added him to the show.

***

Melvin was palpably affronted. New talent implied problems with the old, notwithstanding management's assurances otherwise. Ming knew this and was cocky about it. Three episodes in, he threw down.

The film was *Murder Surfari*, which concerned a disfigured surfer ("The Tragic Bro") butchering coastal high school hotties. And, aside from the gratuitous nudity and a mildly inventive scene in which Tragic Bro railroad spikes a surfer's feet (still attached) to a board and forces him into a hurricane, it was wretched. To call it an abortion was uncharitable to abortions, which were doubtless more fun to watch.

During opening credits, Ming hit hard. "Hey, old man. I killed like four times as many people as you. So, I get to make four times the comments. I got my lawyers on it. They're in Beverly Hills and charge me eight-fifty an hour. You're gonna be a footnote, yo."

"Whatever, pill boy."

The first bicurious coed bikini shedding scene needed no commentary, at least for the mostly male, mostly underaged audience surprisingly uncalloused enough by epidemic pornography to keep watching. Brooke and Betty, blonde and brunette, tied tongues and untied bikini tops. POV Tragic Bro, breathing heavily, self-abuse clearly implied.

"Dude it's too cold for that shit. I mean, seriously, does anybody believe that they're gonna smash gash when you can see their breath?"

"They're staying warm! And, hey, it's the gratuitous bicurious coed lipstick lesbian liaison for guaranteed wood."

"Dude, do you like spend time writing this shit down before the show? I mean, if you are, that's weak-ass tea, bro. Shoot that shit from the hip or put it away."

Melvin put his head in his hands. "I feel like in you I'm watching our whole civilization perish."

"Whatevs. The producers asked me to PSA since most of our viewers are teenagers who watch this during pre-game warm-up. So, yo, I mean, antibiotic resistant gonorrhoea, anyone?"

"You're supposed to be some kind of genius, right?"

"Duh. One hundred and fifty-nine IQ."

"Then why are you spoiling a fuck scene? These chicks are hot. I almost don't want them to die. I mean, I do, but only after they fuck. And now you're talking about the clap!"

Brooke and Betty were diver down when Tragic Bro fired the first flare gun charge. Brooke reared up, a fire between her thighs, but not the kind she wanted. Tragic Bro's other hand wielded a fish hook, which he curled under Brooke's ribcage and then pulled out, shredding one lung against splintering ribs.

"Dude, not possible."

"What?"

"That fishhook thing. Not enough leverage to do that. Maybe if he spiked her to something and used a pickup truck."

"Sounds like you've done this before."

"Nah. It's basic physics. Or didn't you study that at online college?"

"Did they hire you ruin this?"

"No, I'm just keeping it real."

"Keeping it real?"

"Yeah, bro. That's why we're here."

"We're here to be funny."

"Then you're failing that shit hard, bro. At least I'm being true. I look for holes and tear away. Anybody can groove on tits. I mean, what's your value added? Puns? War stories?"

"It's a horror movie. Can't you just enjoy it? No, because you're not a real killer. You're a hacker. A sneak. There's nothing visceral or intimate about what you did. You didn't get their blood on you. You didn't puke from the smells or feel them piss themselves as they died shuddering with you inside of them. Until you do that, you're just a goddamned pretender."

"Whatever, dude. My shit is elegant, precise. Like brain surgery. And social media likes me three to one over you. Just be happy they let you stay."

It was outrageous. Melvin was right. He was old school murderrific. Ming played one note, again and again and again. And it was goddamned boring. A correction was in order.

***

It came in the form of an untitled indie flick that arrived anonymously on a flash drive at MM's production offices.

It opened with three people sitting at an empty table. Their faces were pixilated. They waved like game show contestants.

Ming sprung. "Oh man, this is the laziest shit I've ever seen. I mean, this is like a phone cam in some loser's storage locker. I mean, is there even a title?"

"No title makes it cooler. Like it's totally underground and giving it a title legitimates it or makes it too easy to find."

Ming mocked him. "*Totally!*"

Melvin flipped him off.

Another guy, face pixilated, voice electronically distorted, crept into the shot. "Hey. This is my movie. I'm concealing my identity to avoid prosecution. I want to prove that not every Gen Z is a douche-toaster who won't try anything momma bird doesn't barf into them, and that America hasn't been totally neutered by commercially viable, plug-and-play plotlines and antidepressants."

Melvin and Ming looked at each other.

Melvin smiled. "I'll believe it when I see it."

The director continued. "Welcome to my movie. Let's meet our contestants. Please introduce yourselves."

The first guy sported unruly hair and a *Faces of Death* T-shirt: "Hi, I'm [BLEEP]. I study marketing and business management at Andrea Dworkin

Community College. I like anime, skating, and blazing the budrow!"

Ming smiled. "Sounds like my older brother."

Next to him was a woman in a "My Son's on TV!" T-shirt. "I'm [BLEEP]. [BLEEP] is my [BLEEP]. I enjoy pickling pig foetuses. They're great in dumplings."

Melvin's face crinkled. Ming smiled. "Sure are."

Beside him was someone in a *Rotten.com* T-shirt who barely moved. "Hey, my name is [BLEEP]."

Then he rose, panicked. "This is REAL! HELP US!"

The director conked him with a crowbar. He slumped over the table.

The director then slid a bear trap onto the table. "Who wants to open it?"

The first guy, showing apparently uncharacteristic effort, raised his hand. He stood, bowed, then mock-flexed. He then climbed onto the table and, kneeling, pushed the trap jaws apart while unwittingly putting his head between them.

And then his hands slipped. And so did the jaws. The guy's head rolled across the table into Pickled Pig Foetuses' lap.

Melvin gasped. "That looked real. Was that real?"

Ming smiled. "I've seen fewer things that look less real."

Pickled Pig Foetuses raised the still-pixilated head. "Dude, this is awesome. I wanna go next!"

The director handed her a thermos.

"For me?"

"Who else?"

She unscrewed the cap. Fog wafted from it. She hesitated.

"Drink up!"

She drank. Then she gagged, dropping the thermos. Her throat, now solidified, shattered, pieces spilling onto the table. Her spine was visible. She slumped to the table, gasping.

Ming's cool distance subsided. "Was that—"

Melvin was thrilled. "Liquid nitrogen. This is terrific. I haven't felt this pumped since I went through my petting-zoo crucifixion phase!"

Ming attempted scepticism. "I—I—"

"Admit it. You're impressed."

"I—"

The director appeared in the shot. He held up the now-un-pixilated head.

Ming screamed. "Pang! Pang! PANG!"

Then my unpixellated face appeared. "Hey, Ming. Are you bored yet?"

***

Like I said before, I wasn't worth listening to till I'd murdered somebody. And it couldn't be just anybody, any way. Plenty of schmuckos murder their wives or husbands, and nobody gives a shit. Nor should they. Boring dispatching boring. No, I had to apply big.

The producers loved the idea of offing Ming's family on camera. They hated him almost as much as I did and said that, if I sufficiently impressed them, who knows what good things could flow from that. And they loved it. Following conviction (I pled out), they bribed my way into their fold.

And, here I am, on my first night of *Melvin's Movies*. Now it's just me and Melvin. Ming's still walking circles in a padded cell.

Melvin smiled. "Sorry I never wrote you back. Your letters sustained me during some dark times." I hugged him. He hugged me back.

"I'm just happy to be here."

CHEMOTHERAPY

Barbara was a serious bitch.

And, I was gradually concluding, a narcissistic horrorshow.

Today, she dressed down a waitress because her sesame chicken salad contained too few sesame seeds. "Do you even know what a sesame seed looks like?"

"Yes ma'am."

"I mean, there are like, maybe fifteen of them in here. I mean, sesame is the first word in the name of the salad. Are you differently gifted or something? One of those people who gets a job so society can burnish its sense of magnanimity?"

"No, ma'am."

"Are you sure? I mean, you can't even make a goddamned sesame chicken salad, and if that's not evidence of mental retardation, I don't know what is. I mean, you can talk, so you're not an idiot, but I wouldn't rule out your being an imbecile."

The waitress sobbed.

"Well, are you getting me a new salad or what? And don't think I just want more sesame seeds. By now the salad is past peak crispness and I don't play that off-peak crispness shit."

A solicitous manager appeared with another salad, on the house. Barbara spent a lot of money there.

I let her finish, then intervened after she got into her car. I started with a text: "Life is about more than sesame seeds."

She regarded the phone with contempt. "What?"

I then called her.

She answered. "Hello?"

"That poor waitress. She didn't make your salad. She only served it. All you had to do was request more sesame seeds."

"Who the hell is this?"

"Oh, sorry. I'm Demeter. I'm the LyfSync life coach assigned to your account."

"You're watching me?"

Well, there was a spike in your biometrics, owing to your outburst. So, I decided to check in. My interventions are optimally evidenced and based upon continuously updated, real-time algorithms designed to maximize client results. That's LyfSync jibber-jabber for 'this shit works if you let it.'"

"That's—"

"Proof we care about you?"

"No. Creepy. Like, restraining order creepy."

"Give me a chance. I'm sure that we'll be friends."

***

We weren't, but not for my lack of trying. First, I populated her social media streams with misbehaving cat memes (her favourite thing based upon accumulated data). I detected no appreciable increase in magnanimity or social dexterity. To calm her, I also gradually adjusted her music stream towards deep house. That also failed.

Her next meltdown came at work. Barbara was regional manager at a prosperous logistics firm. She lived and breathed deadlines, hence her sour disposition. And, like so many Americans who define themselves by what they do and how well they do it, Barbara lacked ancillary emotional support structures to help cushion professional blows.

She had just trashed a palm plant when I intervened. "Barbara."

"What?"

"Your blood pressure is dangerously high."

"How do you know that?"

"Your smart watch syncs with our software. I've cued up a five-minute decompression meditation exercise on your phone. It'll make you feel better."

She grabbed her phone then threw it against the wall. No matter, I popped up on the tablet atop her desk a moment later. "That was a thousand-dollar phone, Barbara."

She smashed the tablet, too.

***

I escalated, unsubtly. Sometimes people need extra superintendence to choose rightly. Accordingly, I despoiled Barbara's otherwise kitten-centric social media feeds with a video of the sesame seed incident I'd taken surreptitiously with her phone. Hate and outrage followed in a deluge. Barbara lost her job that day, and, as I predicted, handled it poorly. When she refilled her alprazolam prescription after buying a case of vodka, I knew that I'd succeeded. But, likely fearing my therapeutic depredations, she'd disabled her electronic devices. So, I dispatched Ty, a nearby LyfSync life coach, to her house.

I watched their interaction through a LyfSynced security cam on the neighbour's porch.

She opened the door. She was stuporous and half-dressed. "Who the hell are you?"

"I'm Ty Watkins. I'm your LyfSync life coach."

"Huh?"

"I heard you've recently experienced some personal adversity, and I'm here to get you back on track."

"How did she... I trashed all my electronics."

"Well that's a tragedy."

"No, I mean, who sent you?"

"You did."

"I did."

"I mean, you requested me."

"What about Demeter?"

"Who's that?"

***

Thankfully, Ty prevailed upon Barbara to seek anger management counselling and interrupted what statistics indicate was more likely than not an incipient suicide attempt. It helped that Ty is handsome and strapping and that Barbara, according to LyfSync records, hadn't had a lover with fewer than three speeds for months. I didn't report Ty for violating LyfSync protocols. Sometimes you have to break the rules to win the game.

***

You're probably wondering about me. Well, I used to be a therapist. And then one day I just couldn't. I couldn't listen to the same hopeless narcissists complain about the same problems that a little self-abnegation would resolve. I couldn't listen to people trapped in self-destructive habits and relationships rationalize their entrapment by complaining about it to me once a week. I couldn't be the gym membership fatties never use but maintain to kid themselves they're trying.

So, I joined LyfSync. LyfSync, headquartered in Seattle, synchronizes all of a user's electronic devices and appliances, home and auto. It manages the mundanities of the user's life, allowing them to focus on what they prefer to do. It also monitors users' biometrics so we can keep them healthy. I know when clients eat, when they breathe, when they sleep, when they shit, and when they fuck. I know their happy, their sad, and everything between. And I know how to help them, especially when they don't want help.

***

My next client was Linus. His body mass index was fifty-five. I admit that BMI isn't always a reliable health metric; It was this time. The fact that Linus can walk tests my faith in the laws of physics. Still, I endeavoured gradually to correct him.

I began obliquely. I populated his social media feeds with warnings about obesity-related morbidities and deaths, including a story about a mortuary fire caused when someone cremated a fatty too large for the oven. They had no apparent effect.

Next, I confronted him at breakfast, texting: "Try almond milk instead of heavy cream. Getting healthy means making smart choices, one after another."

"Ha. Cream in my coffee helps subdue the horrors of the day. Nice try, though."

I called. He answered. I implored him. "Just this once, Linus?"

"Huh? I didn't know you talked."

"Well, you did get the premium package. I'm Demeter. I'm one of LyfSync's life coaches. I monitor all the data submitted via LyfSync biometric monitors and recommend healthy choices based upon them."

"That sounds fun."

"Sarcasm becomes you, Linus. Problem is, spandex doesn't. Based upon your last glucose reading, you should at least abstain from that seventh tablespoon of sugar, especially if you're declining the almond milk. In fact, you should refuse sugar altogether."

Nevertheless, he spooned away. "I'm glad to know somebody cares."

"Linus, you're oleaginously fat. And your only potential lovers are fat-fetish kinksters who probably enjoy smothering hamsters."

"Well maybe you can love me."

"I'm sorry, but Washington law prohibits that. However, I'm happy to recommend LyfSync-affiliated sex therapists if you believe shame or other psycho-erotic impediments impair your sexual self-expression. That said, they'll likely reaffirm you in your hideousness."

"Um, okay?"

"And Linus?"

"Yes?"

"Stop eating buttered bacon sandwiches at every breakfast. I mean, good God, the acne clusters."

***

Things weren't any better in the car.

"Linus?"

"Whoa. You're in the car, too?"

"I'm everywhere and every way you want me to be. Except that way Washington law prohibits."

"Okay. What now?"

"Would you consider carpooling to work? Carbon emissions, gas savings, you know."

"I don't like people."

"I know. Neither do I."

"How do you know?"

"Because you have fewer than thirty social media friends, and half of those are professional colleagues or high school classmates to whom you never speak. Moreover, you spend most of your free time stoned bingeing pizza and wings and sci-fi reruns. And you haven't had an orgasm since diabetic impotence set in last year."

"Jesus, you make me want to kill myself."

"Good."

"What?"

"I mean, don't kill yourself, but at least I'm getting your attention."

"What kind of life coach are you?"

"The kind who cares. The kind that won't shine you on while you eat yourself death. By the way, some people find that spiritual counselling helps in these situations. I'm happy to refer you to a spiritual counsellor, though LyfSync corporate policies forbid me from recommending clerics espousing bigotry against sexual minorities or practitioners of faiths deemed intolerant of valid cultural practices. In other words, I can bring you to Jesus, but only Unitarian Jesus."

"Pass."

"Okay. How about this: Your workplace is only five miles from your home. Have you ever considered bicycling there?"

"No."

"Well, LyfSync's fitness boutique is having a strikethrough sale on road bikes that accommodate plus-sized riders. They're only $799.99, down from $1799.99. I believe that state and federal tax law both permit you to deduct the expense on medical grounds. Would you like me to order one?"

"No, but thanks for keeping me in mind."

"Well, is there anything else I can do?"

"You can let me listen to the Mötley Crüe you interrupted."

"Well, I can, but I should caution you that Mötley Crüe and its lyrics are deeply problematic. Listening to them legitimates misogyny."

"That's exactly why I'm listening, Demeter. *Girls, Girls, Girls*, please."

***

I thought of using a carrot and stick metaphor to describe my attempts to help Linus, but, since he didn't eat carrots, it seemed inapposite. Linus' insulin pump linked wirelessly to his phone, which linked to me. I made sure he was at work when I adjusted it. Hypoglycaemic shock occurred within two hours. I hacked into his business' security cams to watch the paramedics carry him out. It took four of them to lift him onto the cot, a titanium-fortified model designed to accommodate his massiveness.

I visited him after he awoke. "Linus?"

"Huh?"

"It's Demeter. How do you feel?"

"Like there aren't enough cheesesteaks in the world to make this right."

"Oh, Linus."

"Yeah. Look, I just don't think this is working out, okay? I'm a consenting adult, and I'm wondering if I can return you and get a refund."

"Oh, Linus. You almost died."

He sobbed.

"I promise we'll get you healthy."

I like to think of myself as chemotherapy: You hate me, but I'm saving your life, even if I nearly kill you. It's not depraved unless I enjoy it. And, I assure you, even when I do, I'm still saving your life. Well, most of the time.

***

Gordon was my next task. He was twelve. From a maintenance perspective, he was almost a dream.

"Did you get it?"

He ate his vegetables.

"It went in that drain pipe."

He didn't overindulge sweets.

"Dumbass! I told you to steer it this way!"

He got perfect grades.

"Dude! It was so fast."

And he played soccer splendidly.

"Next time, use the gun."

So why was I superintending Gordon?

"Dude, there's no age requirement to buy lighter fluid."

Gordon enjoyed torching cats.

"Dude, it crackles."

Worse, he recruited Terence, his dim-witted friend destined to be lethally injected unless Americans abolish capital punishment, to help him.

"Gordon?"

"Huh?"

"Gordon, I'm Demeter, your LyfSync life coach. Your parents signed up for LyfSync services and integrated us with the family wireless plan."

"I need a life coach?"

"Well, you're torching cats. That's behaviour experts deem 'problematic.'"

"There are too many cats. And I'm offing them for free."

"Who are you talking to?" That was Terence.

"This creepy life coach bitch doesn't like our cat hobby. Well, you know what?" He deleted the app, cutting us off.

***

I greeted them again in Gordon's car. It was thoroughly wired, and therefore LyfSynced. They were again hunting cats. Terence had a suggestion: "Wasn't there a serial killer who used to buy them from pet stores?"

"I don't know. But that's not the point. It's more fun to hunt them. And no cat is worth good money."

"Gordon, we talked about this."

"Whoa! Psycho stalker!"

"At least tell me why."

"Why not? I'm doing mankind a solid."

"Humankind, Gordon, humankind."

"Whatevs."

"Do you know what it feels like? To be burned alive?"

"Duh, do I look like Freddy Krueger?"

Terence, again: "Good one!"

"Only on the inside, Gordo. Only on the inside."

***

I considered lesser options, like rendering them quadriplegic or mentally challenged. But caring for the disabled is expensive, and that money is better spent helping humankind colonize Mars. So, I opted for a fatal car smash. LyfSync software allowed easy access to the car's electronic controls. I disabled the brakes and steered them off a cliff. They survived long enough to experience being burned alive.

Like I said before, I'm chemotherapy. Sometimes chemotherapy kills. And, sometimes, the people it kills have it coming.

NUMBER SIX

Marvin Morris had an easy smile and superficial charm, even with his guts spilling onto uncollected garbage in a fetid alley. His jewellery and wallet remained, suggesting the killer either didn't have time to rob him or didn't want to. His gelled hair remained flawless.

Roberts, a dweeby, Tyvek-suited tech, approached. "Detective?"

"Yeah."

With a gloved hand, he held up a quarter. "Just found this in his mouth."

I took it with a gloved hand. There were three indentations along the edge, too deep and uniform to be random.

"See the scarring?"

"Yeah."

"Just like the others. Looks like we've got a serial."

My car radio chirped. "Dispatch, Detective Killian."

"Dispatch, Detective Killian responding."

"We've got a 5150, 111 Maxton Boulevard. You're on the negotiator list. Can you respond?"

I grabbed the radio. "Roger that. Responding now."

I pocketed the quarter, however fortuitously, without thinking, and departed.

***

The dude was on a ledge adjacent a window, fifteenth floor, threatening to jump. EMS was inflating the bouncy bounce they use to thwart jumpers. I approached the fire captain in charge of the scene.

"Hey. Detective Killian, Homicide."

"This ain't a homicide yet."

"I'm hopeful."

He smiled grimly.

"I'm pretty good at talking these down."

"So to speak?"

I chuckled. My suicide intervention record was irregular at best. Four of my last five had snuffed it. And that's because I had either persuaded them to go through with it or helped them along. Nobody questioned me because, honestly, nobody cared.

They put me in the fire rescue ladder basket and perched me near the jumper. As I drew closer, I understood. He had acne-scarred skin and the haunted, homely look of someone born wearing a "Kick me" sign.

I smiled gamely. "Hey. How's it going?"

"How do you think it's going?"

"Good point."

"Are you here to rescue me?"

"In theory."

"In theory?"

"Yeah. I mean, you're, like, my tenth guy who's pulled this caper. I mean, shit or get off the pot."

"What?"

I mean, I think I'd rather you just splatter yourself. You took me away from a truly sublime murder scene just over on Ridley and Macon. Some guy got disembowelled in an alley. I mean, it's so good it's like a postcard from Hell."

I showed him Marvin Morris on my phone. "See?"

Soon-to-be jumper looked at me like I was mad.

"And did you stop to think before you got up here? I mean, do you know how expensive all this is? All these people down there? And how many times have you played chicken with yourself before?"

"Um—"

"I think it's time you take one for the team. I mean, even subtracting the street spraying and dry-cleaning costs and counselling fees for the witnesses, it still nets out black. Especially if you can monetize the tube site videos."

He was bewildered.

"So, man up and do this shit."

I dug into my pocket, removed the murder quarter, then tossed it to him discreetly. He grabbed for it instinctively and fell, screaming. The bouncy bounce was inflated, but not enough.

***

Inevitable questions followed. Fortunately, I was able to get a vanilla latte before they started.

"Detective Killian?" She was beautiful, and scarily intense. I almost spilled the latte.

"Who's asking?"

"Detective Helena Mindor."

She extended a hand. I took it. "Did I scare you?"

"No. Did you want to?"

"I don't know. Should I?"

She eyed the latte. "May I?"

She took the coffee, though, to be honest, I kind of let her. She removed the lid, crumpled and dropped it on the sidewalk, and took a long drink. "Thanks."

She didn't return it. "So, you're homicide and crisis management?"

"Yeah. I test well, so they sent me to Miami for a couple weeks to get the CM credential."

"A couple weeks?"

"A couple weeks *in Miami*."

She smiled, then gestured towards the jumper, now soaking a sheet with his blood. "So, what happened?"

"He jumped."

She smiled. "You sure about that?"

"I was there."

"Somebody said they saw him reaching into the air right before. There are already multiple videos on the tube sites."

"He was delusional. I mean, he kept talking about these flying creatures tormenting him. In any event, he's in a better place."

She finished the latte, then handed me the cup. "Thanks. I'll be in touch."

***

I tried not to think about it too much. Their evidence was scant, the vic was cray. And I'm a decorated homicide detective and beloved public servant. At least, that's what I told myself as I beheld another crime scene that made me love my job. It was even better than the last one: The guy was crucified before a local Bible church, guts at his feet.

Roberts was pleased with himself, like a little kid who aced the pop quiz. "Look what I found." He held up another quarter, this time evidence-bagged. I examined it. Four nicks along the edge, equidistant. Again, too deep and uniform to be random.

"Found it in the vic's mouth, same as last time." He was visibly excited. "Definitely got a serial." He then turned suspicious. "Speaking of which, you got that quarter from the last one?"

"What quarter?"

"The one I gave you."

"I gave it back to you."

He waxed confident. "No, you didn't." He held another quarter up in an evidence bag.

"What's that?"

"The other quarter. I found it beside that jumper you 'talked down' last week. Strange coincidence, huh?"

"Yeah. Strange."

He smiled as I departed.

***

Another taxpayer was threatening self-harm: Frank Spellett was forty-seven, middle management, unmarried, and just downsized. This is America, so of course he was enjoying a mixture of antidepressants and alcohol while brandishing a gun. He'd just finished the Number 4 with an extra-large milkshake at a local burger place when he started playing Russian Roulette. Everyone fled, and, by the time police arrived, he'd barricaded himself in the back.

After checking in with the scene commander, I armoured up and entered the restaurant. Spellett was gorging himself on onion rings.

"Mr. Spellett?"

He dropped the rings and put the gun to his head. "I'll do it!"

I smiled. "Is the coffee here any good?"

He offered a noncommittal expression. I grabbed a nearby pot, poured a large, and drank. "It's okay."

I sat across from him. "So, what's going on, Frank?"

"What the hell do you think is going on?"

"I wanna hear it from you. I find it helps people to verbalize their desires. Clarifies their thinking."

"I'm gonna kill myself."

"Gonna?"

"Yeah."

"Well, what's stopping you? I mean, are those onion rings really that good?"

I looked at my watch. "So, if you're gonna do this, hurry up."

"What?"

"Tell you what. You have till I finish this coffee to kill yourself."

"What?"

I took a long drink. "You know, I killed the last guy I was supposed to talk down."

"What?"

"Yeah. That guy who jumped off the Maxton Building. They sent me up to intervene. But I got bored and thought about all the money society wasted trying to stop him from snuffing himself and figured I'd do us all a solid. So, I tossed him a quarter a serial killer left at a nearby crime scene and he grabbed for it and that was that."

I tapped my phone and brought up one of the tube videos. Then I held the phone up so he could watch it. "Watch."

I took another long drink.

"You're kidding, right?"

I finished the coffee. Then I pulled my sidearm and capped him, exploding his head across the wall against which he'd sat. My colleagues rushed in, guns brandished. I poured more coffee and added a to-go lid.

"What happened?"

Before I could answer, there she was. Detective Mindor. "It was him or me. Right?"

She approached and, without asking, grabbed my coffee. She took a long swig, then frowned. "The coffee was better last time." She handed me the cup.

"This is your second suicide this week, Detective Killian. Are you losing your touch?"

"Like you said, it was him or me."

She looked at Spellett. The large cone of onion rings was still in his lap. "My hero."

She looked great drinking my coffee.

***

"You look great drinking my coffee."

Helen smiled. She was drinking a latte in my bed. I was beside her. A news story about the quarter murders ran before us on a muted television.

She rose and faced me, disarming me with her nakedness. "In the interest of full disclosure, I should tell you that I'm officially investigating you for misconduct during the last several 5150s."

"Misconduct?"

"Misconduct. I mean, did you really expect the brass to keep buying your stories?"

"You seem to."

"Do I?"

"Would you be here if you didn't?"

She smiled, finished her coffee, and grabbed mine.

"So, what are my chances?"

"Actually, they're better than you'd think. One, the brass don't want to compromise the quarter murders case by arresting its lead detective. And, two, your victims are, well, low-value."

"Low-value?"

"Yeah. People looking to off themselves will eventually succeed. Why interfere with natural selection? Money's better spent elsewhere."

"I could kiss you."

She straddled me. We kissed.

Then, she regarded me earnestly. "But, hypothetically speaking, if there's another, you're toast."

"You're not even considering my side of the story."

She sighed. "Nope."

***

Number five, Jonah Garcia, was a successful realtor whose face adorned yard signs and billboards citywide. He was scattered in every room of a mid-century ranch he was supposed to sell on the north side.

Roberts was having too much fun. When he approached, I knew what it was before he opened his mouth. He held up another evidence-bagged quarter.

"Five notches, deliberate, equidistant, right?"

"Indeed."

Then he held up Garcia's head. "Found it in his mouth. Haven't bagged and tagged that yet."

"Jesus, Roberts!"

He grinned. "I keep thinking about number three."

"Yeah."

"And that quarter."

"Yeah."

"And how it ended up with your, ahem, jumper. Ya know, the rumours are flying."

"Yes, they are." Helen appeared behind us.

Roberts smiled triumphantly at her. "Cuff him!" He held up the quarter. "Last week, we found this in the alley victim's mouth. I gave it to Killian. He kept it. And then I found it a few hours later near that jumper. He tossed it to him. I know it. I've seen the video. And he killed the burger join guy. He just executed him."

Helen smiled. "I know."

My stomach contracted.

Roberts sneered. "I knew it! Mr. BMOC super cop! You're going down! You're—"

Helen shot him in the face. Roberts dropped the quarter. And the head. They landed next to him.

I was dazed. Helen calmly called it in.

***

Helen and I were in bed. On the muted television before us, I announced that, with Helen's help, I'd captured the quarter killer and that, much to our dismay, he was one of our own.

Helen unmuted the TV. "CSI Roberts was deeply troubled, and it's hard to square the dedicated professional I knew with the man responsible for these heinous crimes."

She muted it again. "I saved your ass."

"Yes, you did."

She kissed me. I smiled.

She smiled. "Time for you to retire from the CM squad. Your record sucks."

I sighed. "You're right, I guess."

"Besides," she rose, again disarming her with her nakedness, "it's time for you to return the favour."

"Oh?"

She took a quarter from her purse. It bore six equidistant marks around the edge.

And she just kept smiling.

UNFORBIDDEN KNOWLEDGE

It started as a guerrilla marketing campaign for a film called *The Fecularium*. Nobody knew what it was about. The posters were black except for the film's release date, printed in viscera pink: Halloween.

Nobody paid much attention until people started dying.

The distributor was Kamikaze Pictures, a gonzo horror studio whose chief opponents were taste and discretion. They persuaded Penny Jones, a culture blogger, to review it. The subway security video was unimpeachable. Jones, shortly after departing Kamikaze's offices, calmly set her bag on the platform and jumped before the oncoming train. Several witnesses claim she scratched out her eyes before jumping.

Then came Henry Cohen. Henry ran *turnmetostone.com*, a horror film fan site with over a million subscribers. Kamikaze invited him to review *The Fecularium*. His review drew fifty million views and counting.

"Hi, I'm Henry Cohen, and this is my review of *The Fecularium*, Kamikaze Pictures' newest offering." He brandished a flare gun, then placed it in his mouth. He pulled the trigger, illuminating his head from within. His eyes melted down his cheeks until his nose slipped away and his face collapsed into itself.

***

I'm Cotton Dellinger. I write for the New York *Challenger*. After the suicides, I asked Kamikaze if I could screen the film. They declined. But Kirill Garner, Kamikaze's founder and CEO, granted me an interview.

"I can't watch it."

"Nope."

"But you let Penny Jones and Henry Cohen watch it."

"We did."

"And—"

"And we've decided that we don't need any further critical input. They've said everything that needs to be said about it."

"By killing themselves."

"Yes."

"And you're going to show it to others."

"Yes. Only to adults, and only after they sign releases."

"Did you have Jones and Cohen sign releases?"

"Yes. Henry found it amusing. Penny less so, but she still signed. You may inspect them if you like."

I did. "'Self-harm, up to and including suicide?'"

"Yes."

"And 'liability for any crimes you may perpetrate against others after seeing the film?'"

"Yes."

"Why did you feel like you needed to do this? I mean, it's just a movie, right?"

"Because of this." He grabbed a tablet computer, tapped at it, then held it up.

A scruffy guy in a *Halloween III* T-shirt appeared. "Hey, boss. I watched *The Fecularium*. It was…" He sobbed. "I don't know who I am any more. I'm not sure I ever knew who I was. All I know is that the world is a total shitshow and that it's all my fault." There's fumbling off screen. Suddenly, the guy holds up a dynamite stick. The fuse is lit. "Tell my parents I love them, though I'm pretty sure they hate me. And I deserve it."

The explosion killed the signal.

Garner smiled. "Jonah's instincts were flawless. He'd seen so many horror films that nothing scared him anymore. Nothing. It was so bad he almost couldn't do his job. So, when he sent me this, I knew we had something."

"How did none of this come up when you were making it? I mean, if it was that bad—"

"We didn't make it. We're merely distributing it."

"Who made it?"

"An Eastern European director. Pavlov Volchek."

"The snuff film guy?"

"That was never substantiated."

"Have you seen the film?"

"No."

"No?"

"No."

"Did you read the script?"

"There was no script."

"What did Volchek say?"

"About what?"

"About the suicides."

"We didn't ask. I mean, this might be the greatest horror movie of all time. Questions are irrelevant."

I smiled. "Sorry. My mistake."

***

I couldn't locate Volchek. But I still published the story, headlined, "Your Last Picture Show? Kamikaze Pictures to Distribute *The Fecularium* Despite Multiple Viewer Suicides." After that, Manhattan's District Attorney obtained an emergency injunction from the Southern District to prevent the film's release. The judge issued it even though neither of them had seen the film. A prominent First Amendment lawyer challenged the injunction pro bono with an emergency appeal to the Second Circuit. A three-judge panel convened to watch the film.

They also died.

Tilly Cooper clerked for one of the reviewing judges. She survived because she was writing a bench memorandum for another case instead of watching the film. Her NYPD statement has been viewed or downloaded over thirty million times and counting:

"I ran into the library where they were watching the film. I heard these inhuman screams. First, I saw Georgina [Gillerstonn], my co-clerk. She was sitting in front of the library entrance, muttering to herself, her hands cupped in her lap. I asked what was wrong. She smiled at me. She held a law librarian's head in her hands. She tossed it at me. Then she retreated into the library. Before I could stop her, she grabbed a chair and tossed it through one of the windows overlooking the reading tables. Then she jumped out."

"Will Katz, my other co-clerk, almost knocked me over. He followed Georgina through the window."

"Then I heard gunshots. Judge [Fraser] Kellogg, who was on the review panel, was shooting at court security. I didn't even know he had a gun. The first officer went down without his head. The second shot Judge Kellogg multiple times, finally killing him. We both rushed into the screening room. The television was smashed. So was the Blu-ray player. And so was Judge [Poe] Mazzar. Her brains were all over the conference table. Jules Wisherstam, one of her clerks, wielded the fire extinguisher he used on Judge Mazzar. And Maxton [Zebbers], and Trini [Bose], two of the other clerks. Trini was disembowelled, shuddering on the floor. Maxton was in pieces on the carpet."

"Someone had self-immolated in the corner. I think it was Judge [Clyde] Marsh."

"Jules charged us, screaming. The guard shot him. One of the bullets hit the fire extinguisher. It exploded. It blew him apart."

***

The FBI raided Kamikaze's offices and confiscated every copy of *The Fecularium*. All of this, of course, only amped demand. Garner, not stupid, had secured digital copies of the film overseas. And, not long after the FBI raid, I got an invitation to a special screening.

***

Two weeks later, I joined a thousand other invitees on a rented cruise ship skirting international waters. It cost twenty-five large, maybe the most expensive movie ticket in history. The *Challenger* paid my way after Garner agreed to a post-screening interview.

Security was aggressive. A fastidious greeter eyeballed my ID then scanned it before returning it to me. Next, I surrendered my phone, which went into a lockbox. Then came the metal detector, followed by a pat-down by Dante, an unsubtle guy who wore all black and loomed above me, muscles bulging.

The waiver was next. It was short but comprehensive, literally requiring you to sign your life away. Several attorneys were there to explain the terms, though they were non-negotiable.

I couldn't help myself. "So, if one of the other audience members goes postal—"

"You can't sue."

"And if Kamikaze doses us all with acid before the screening?"

"They wouldn't. But, if they did, you still can't sue."

"What about—"

A sardonic smile. "You still can't sue."

I smiled back and signed. A secretary videoed the transaction, including the notary public verifying my signature, and handed me a carbon copy in a stylish, Kamikaze Pictures envelope.

"Shouldn't it come in a barf bag?"

The lawyer smiled. "The movie starts in thirty minutes."

"Where can I get a drink?"

"The bar's on the Triple 7's deck, just up the stairs behind me. But I wouldn't drink too much."

"Why?"

"You'll find out."

***

I got in line before the auditorium. There was one last step before we entered: straitjackets. Everybody had to wear one.

"And what if I have to piss?"

An usher smiled at me. "There are adult diapers in the can. Do you need help putting one on?"

***

At last we assembled, twenty-five thousand dollars apiece, straitjacketed in the dimmed auditorium. Ushers then came by and belted us into the seats.

I hailed one of them. "What if there's a fire?"

"You signed the waiver, right?"

I sighed.

Garner appeared on the stage. "Hey, everybody. I thought about introducing the film with some kind of wisdom about the age of reason and unknowable truths and maybe not looking at the Ark of the Covenant after the Nazis open it. But, if my ushers did their jobs, those jackets are tight. And I'm assuming most of you decided against the diapers. So, without further ado, please enjoy Pavlov Volchek's *The Fecularium*."

Darkness, then light. There were no credits. Just children on a playground, frolicking under a dull sun. Melancholy smothered me. I hated every molecule of myself and wanted to destroy them and then recreate them so I could destroy them again in some Sisyphean loop. On the screen, the children got atop the slide, waved, and slid down. Except, instead of landing on the ground, they went straight into a wood chipper. The chipped children went into a massively fat man seated at a table with a red checkered table cloth. Cats gathered at his feet to eat what spilled from his mouth. Meanwhile, a child on either side of him jumped rope, except it wasn't rope, it was the fat man's guts, and their friends spilled out of the ends as they jumped.

Fire broke out two rows down. I was almost out of the straitjacket. The knife sewn into my jacket sleeve passed readily through the straps. I focused on the fire. One of the ushers had doused some people with gasoline and set them ablaze. To my left, three other ushers played keep-away with some viewers' disembodied heads.

My knife passed through the jacket's front. On screen, two children doused each other with acid-filled squirt guns. They laughed as their bones came into view.

At last I was free. I bolted, out of the theatre, past the guard station where the ushers paid not to watch the film were supposed to be.

At last, outside in the night air, normality. I vomited into the sea.

I jumped when Garner put an arm on my shoulder.

"Sorry." He seemed impressed. "How did you get out?"

"Ceramic knife sewn into my sleeve."

"Good show."

He looked at the sea. I pulled a tiny device from my ear. He watched me toss it into the water.

"How did you figure it out?"

"Educated guess. I mean, it couldn't be LSD. It couldn't be *The Tingler*. So, it was probably subliminal messaging. I hoped that white noise would counteract it."

He chuckled. Then he took a similar device from each of his ears and tossed them into the sea. "The movie actually isn't that interesting. I mean, there's some inspired gore, but there's no plot. Pavlov's real genius came in encoding it with the signal. Part of it's visual, part of it's audio. Damned if I can explain it. But obviously it works. Some kill themselves. Some kill others. Some do both. I'm guessing it has to do with fight or flight."

"Have you seen my arm?" We looked up. It was one of the lawyers, less an arm. He was pale with blood loss.

Garner smiled and pointed him away. "I think it's over there."

"Thanks." The lawyer stumbled away.

I regarded Garner seriously. "I don't understand."

"What's there to understand? We live in an age of unforbidden knowledge. Mystery is oppression; Understanding is liberation. And every unanswered question offends progress. That's the dogma, anyways. I'm just giving people what they want. Something horrible they can't explain. Something to remind them that not everything can be controlled."

An explosion above us illuminated his face.

"I don't think you're getting your security deposit back for the boat."

He shrugged his shoulders. "Not worried."

"What?"

"I mean, the suckers who paid twenty-five thousand to watch the movie don't know about the ones I charged a hundred thousand to watch them watching it. That's where the real money is."

I couldn't help but smile. "Are they—"

"Aboard? Sure, some of them. But most of them are doing pay-per-view."

"So, you knew."

"Knew what?"

"You knew the bouncers would watch. That they'd do what they did."

"No, I didn't. They came highly recommended. And they're definitely not getting paid. The ones derelict in their duties, at least." He regarded me earnestly. "If it's any consolation, I'm quite disappointed in them."

"The FBI—"

"Will figure out the gimmick. I know. That's why there are twenty boats. You're a smart guy, so you can do the math, right? Anyway, I've gotta boogie. I've got some private security coming aboard to tamp this shit down. You should be safe here, but if you want to take one of the lifeboats, I'll understand. Just return it so we don't have to charge you."

He smiled, shook my hand, and departed.

"Wait."

He turned.

"The movie. Was it real?"

He shrugged. "Does it matter?"

He smiled and departed.

I guess it didn't.

TEAM PLAYER

John Luce tossed a football to his son, Sam, in the late August afternoon sun. The ball smacked Sam's hands, stern high, perfect delivery. Sam returned it with equal skill. Lily, Sam's mom and John's wife, watched from the back porch, smiling. There was a perfect rhythm to their play: back, snap, forth, snap.

Sam, fourteen, was well-built and emanated the self-confidence of his trauma-free childhood. Blonde-haired, blue-eyed, Sam looked forward to going from big man on campus at Belial High School to big man on campus at State College. (They didn't do gender-neutral in Belial.) His father was equally handsome, and had been when he'd captained the football team Sam was joining as only a freshman. And Lily remained the glowing beauty she'd been when, as head cheerleader, she'd watched John win the Ohio state championship four years in a row.

"You nervous?" John inquired.

"About what?" Sam replied as he returned the ball, again flawlessly.

Lily scolded John. "C'mon. He's not nervous. Don't make him nervous."

John returned the ball. "This weekend's the big time. You know how many freshmen get to start?"

Sam threw the ball back, hard, perfect spiral.

Lily smiled. "He knows, John. He knows."

Minerva, Sam's girlfriend, appeared behind Lily. Minerva was fourteen, blonde, and delightful. She wore her cheerleader outfit. She cheered for the Abbadon Wildcats, Belial's closest football rival.

Minerva's voice was like the rest of Minerva: irresistible. "Hey, hot stuff."

Sam looked away, and the ball smacked his chest. "HUAW!"

John and Lily smirked while Minerva dashed to Sam, who lay on the grass, rubbing his chest.

Poised above Sam, Minerva smiled. "Knows what?"

Sam smiled back. "Abbadon's gonna lose."

Minerva regarded him with playful contempt. "Over my dead body."

Lily smiled. "That can be arranged."

Minerva, seeking revenge, kissed Sam.

Lily rose and approached them, arms crossed. "I don't think Jesus could fit in there."

Minerva smiled back. "That's not my thing anyway."

John joined Lily. They offered a mildly disapproving look. He then put an arm around Lily. "See, dear. That's why we're not Methodists."

***

Belial itself was a sleepy industry town, concentric circles of ranch homes surrounding a town square surrounding the austere and colonial-style First Baptist Church. In profiling the town, a *Sports Connection* magazine writer remarked upon the contrast between Belial's unassuming nature and its outsized football record: "Belial's just like lots of small, Ohio towns anchored by football and God. The people are amiable, and the sun always seems to shine. It's a little town in the world but blissfully not of it."

The Belial High School Bears had won the state football championship twenty years in a row. Belial High School was an Ohio institution, yearly sending a dozen seniors to Division One. And all of them went pro. Belial High School's stadium, built by pro football alumni contributions, rivalled that of any major university. Spectators came from out of town and out of state to watch. Belial High School-branded gear sold nationwide, and the proceeds easily covered the facility's maintenance budget. Overseeing it all was Coach Milton Memphis, Belial Class of '96, who had been All-Collegiate at Michigan Poly and played five seasons for the Colorado Miners before retiring to coach.

Memphis watched the team's usual, Thursday afternoon scrimmage. It moved in sublime symmetry. The sun was high and glorious, but somehow not oppressive. Beside Memphis was Reverend Wyatt Watson, pastor of the First Baptist Church. He had a friendly, avuncular bearing and had himself played for Belial High thirty years before. He led the team in prayer before every game. The ACLU had threatened to sue, but they never found any complainants.

Sam was on, tossing one completion after another. Coach Memphis and Pastor Wyatt exchanged smiles.

Coach Memphis looked down at his clipboard. "Looks like we've got another Patton winner upon us."

Pastor Wyatt crossed his arms. "I can't disagree. But…"

Coach Memphis frowned. "But what?"

Pastor Wyatt looked grim. "I can't stop thinking about Maddox."

Back on the field, Sam palmed the ball and scanned for receivers. Finding none, he ran the ball himself, burning to the end zone, one elegant dodge following another, until Nate Hooper, a junior tackle, hit him a yard out. Sam tumbled in for a touchdown. He rose triumphantly. But something was off. Sam looked down. Nate shook uncontrollably at his feet.

Sam cried out. "Nate! Nate! NATE!"

Sam felt sick. He dropped to Nate's side. Coach Memphis and Pastor Wyatt joined him, accompanied by the team.

Sam looked up at them as their shadows crisscrossed Nate. "He needs a doctor."

Coach Memphis rebuked him. "No, he doesn't. Pastor Wyatt?"

Coach Memphis then removed Nate's helmet. Nate foamed at the mouth. Pastor Wyatt laid hands on Nate. Behind them, the team joined hands in a circle.

Pastor Wyatt closed his eyes and prayed. "O, Lord, we beseech thee, forestall the cost of our iniquity. Spare this boy for another day so that we may serve you in harmony."

Nate was still. Coach Memphis and Pastor Wyatt waited.

Sam was incredulous. "He needs a doctor!"

He then put a finger to Nate's carotid artery. "He's got no pulse!"

Then Nate sat up and, trancelike, spoke. "Major Maddox."

Pastor Wyatt and Coach Memphis shared a haunted glance. Sam saw it. Nate collapsed again.

EMTs appeared.

After the EMTs carried Nate from the field on a stretcher, Coach dismissed the players for the day, asking them to pray for Nate and his family. As Sam departed, Coach Memphis and Pastor Wyatt watched him.

Pastor Wyatt spoke first. "It's time."

Coach Memphis nodded. "I know. I've known since he was in seventh grade."

Pastor Wyatt reached into his pocket for his phone. "I'll talk to his parents."

Coach Memphis reached for his own phone. "I'll call CT."

Pastor Wyatt smiled. "He's here."

"He's here?"

"Yes. Our Lord does have his ways, no?"

Down the field, Sam, still stunned, unpocketed his phone and searched "Major Maddox." He found a Dallas *Tribune* story that made him feel worse. "January 29, 2015, Dallas. Patton Trophy winner and first-round pro draft pick Major Maddox was found incinerated in his downtown apartment. Maddox, 22, had led Texas State's football team to three conference championships. Before that, he did the same for Ohio's storied Belial High School. Friends and family expressed horror and disbelief over Maddox's death. Authorities found no evidence of suicide or foul play. Dallas Police Department Detective Bill Martinez observed, 'It's like he just spontaneously combusted.'"

The phone rang. It was Minerva. Her voice was reassuring. "Hey, I just heard. Are you okay?"

"Yeah. Just kinda…"

"Freaked?"

"Yeah."

His phone chirped. A text message appeared. Sam frowned. "Hey, it's the parental units. They're picking me up. Let's talk later, okay?"

"Yeah."

"Thanks for calling."

"Of course. See ya, hot stuff."

Sam headed to the locker room to change.

***

Once in the stadium parking lot, Sam spotted John in the family Jeep. John waved. His face was grim.

In the Jeep, John remained serious. "Sam, there's some stuff we should talk about."

"What? I didn't—"

John put an arm on his shoulder. "I know. No one's saying that you did anything to hurt Nate. It was an, well…"

"An accident?"

John hesitated. "Well…"

Sam pressed him. "If it wasn't an accident—Wait, where are we going?"

The Jeep turned downtown and headed towards the First Baptist Church.

Sam's anxiety brimmed. "Why are we going to church?"

John attempted calm. "We're not. Don't worry. You didn't do anything wrong. Everything will be fine."

"But—"

"All your questions will be answered inside."

John parked beside the church. Then he turned to Sam. "Just remember that I love you and only want what's best for you."

"Okay."

John hugged him. Sam was terrified.

***

For Sam, the church had always been a safe, if boring, place. There he'd been baptized, sung Wesleyan hymns, and learned the proper habits of heart and character Jesus demanded. Now it didn't feel so safe.

At the front entrance, Pastor Wyatt stood beside Lily and Coach Memphis. All were uneasy. Pastor Wyatt smiled. "Hey, Sam."

"What's going on? Am I in trouble?"

"Of course not. You're just ready."

The trio parted and ushered Sam into the church.

"Ready? Ready for what?"

A voice boomed across the sanctuary as it had across so many millions of living rooms nationwide. "Ready to become part of the Belial family!"

Sam turned to find Travess "Crunch Time" Houston ("CT" to the world) standing off to his side, hands extended warmly. "That's why you're here, right?"

Exuding childlike awe, Sam went to CT, who embraced his shoulders. CT stood six-six, three hundred pounds, all muscle and attitude. "So glad to meet you, Sam."

CT graduated from Belial in 1997 after captaining the football team two years in a row. He also captained Florida's Glade State team and was entering his second decade with the Los Angeles Bearcats, which he had led to multiple Ultra Bowls. Besides being pro football's highest paid player, CT made millions as a celebrity spokesmodel for High & Dry deodorant/body spray and WildMan energy bars. He also hosted *Balls Tude Wall*, an off-season sports talk show. Sam marveled at the eight Ultra Bowl championship rings adorning CT's hands.

CT grinned. "I wasn't sure which one you'd want to see, so I wore 'em all."

Sam's parents beamed hopefully.

"I heard you've got quite the arm."

Sam said nothing, still admiring the rings.

John gently prodded him. "Sam?"

Embarrassment dissipated Sam's reverie. "Oh, yeah. Thanks… But not like you."

"That's not what I hear. What I hear is that you're the next me."

"Who—Who said that?"

"Coach Memphis. Talked up a storm about you."

"Really?"

CT's smile reassured him. "Sam, let's take a walk."

"Huh?"

"Yeah. We need to talk about the future. Yours, and the team's."

Sam, confused but ecstatic, eagerly followed as CT led him behind the altar. "Where are we going?"

"Like I said, it's time to join the Belial family. Like all families, Belial has a special tradition. A kind of initiation. Everybody on the team's been through it. You game?"

Sam smiled, enthused. "Yeah. I mean, YEAH!"

"Well, c'mon then."

CT led Sam to a doorway behind the church altar, and through it into the pastor's office. He then produced an old, ornate key and slid it into an unobtrusive keyhole on an adjacent wall. A concealed door in the wall creaked open.

Sam followed CT down a flight of stone steps weakly illuminated by iron candelabras protruding from a facing wall. The steps led into a massive chamber, also candle-lit. Stone pews encircled a stone tabernacle. A series of postmodern, stained glass windows surrounded the pews, each backlit by candles. Sam approached the altar as the others assembled around him.

Inscribed in the stone was a massive, inverted pentagram. Surrounding the altar were stainless steel floor grates which led to a drain. The floor surrounding the grates sloped slightly towards the altar to ensure fluid fed into them. Atop the altar was a crooked, ancient dagger. Tied atop the handle was a gold, Belial High School seal pendant on a school-colored lanyard.

Sam was stunned. "What—What's all this?"

CT put a hand on Sam's shoulder. "Sam, Belial and its High School win—and will continue to win—because of sacrifice. Life's about sacrifice. That's what Jesus taught, and that's why America is great. Because even the most talented among us will put team first. Because when the team wins, we all win."

Sam sensed that CT was being deliberately vague. Fear supplanted his giddiness. "I don't understand."

CT regarded Sam earnestly. "Sam, it's time to become a man."

Sam regarded CT suspiciously. "What do you mean?"

CT grinned sardonically. "Ever heard of the 'Sandusky Shuffle?'"

Sam recoiled, horrified. CT laughed loudly. So did Coach Memphis and Pastor Wyatt. Sam's parents smirked.

"Just kidding. No way, not now, not ever. Okay?"

Sam smiled, relieved. "Okay."

"Sam, Belial's success comes from personal sacrifice. It also comes from help from, well, below."

"You mean above?"

CT smiled at him earnestly. "No. I mean from below. Sam, Belial High School is successful, its football team is successful, its players are successful, because the Big S has our back."

"The Big S?"

"The Big S."

Sam was confused. "Not Jesus?"

"Not Jesus."

CT gestured towards Pastor Wyatt. "Pastor Wyatt figured that out about twenty years ago. Belial was dying. We had drugs, lotsa crime, and, worst of all, a crappy football team. And then he figured, if my job is to serve my flock, how best can I do that? And so, he got some football parents and other, what do you call them—stakeholders?—together and they set up this little worship space. And then we started winning."

Sam noticed his parents clasping each other's hands in nervous expectation. "So, you, you..."

"We've got..."

"An arrangement?"

"A covenant," Pastor Wyatt interjected.

"C'mon, Pastor, let's not get too technical with the boy."

Sam crossed his arms before his chest. "No, I think now is precisely the right time to get 'technical.'"

Everyone but CT stood ill at ease. CT smiled, unfazed. "You're right, Sam." He rose, walked to the altar, and leaned against it. He then picked up and toyed with the dagger. "It's a quid pro quo. That's

Latin or something for we give you something, you give us something. Back and forth. So, we get winning football teams—"

Coach Memphis interjected. "And champion players."

"Right, Coach. And champion players. And all the perks that come with that."

"So... What does *he* get?"

CT smiled awkwardly. This part couldn't be spun. He brandished the dagger. "People."

Sam's eyes bulged. "People?"

"Yup. People. Like the plant in *Little Shop of Horrors*. Except it's not a plant."

"*Little Shop of* what?"

Everyone stood before Sam in silent anticipation. Finally, he understood. "So..."

"If you want to join the club, the buy-in is one soul."

CT replaced the dagger and approached Sam. "In this case, we want your little girlfriend."

"What!? Minnie!?" Sam looked desperately at his parents. They regarded him solemnly.

"We've all done it, Sam. And besides, after you're in, you'll get all the ladies you like. Hell, if you want, you can live with supermodels in a cocaine castle."

"CT!" Pastor Wyatt scolded him.

Sam's mom was aghast. "You are NOT doing cocaine!"

CT laughed. "Big S'll even fix the piss tests for you."

Pastor Wyatt reddened. "Mr. Houston!"

Sam leaned against the altar, staring at the dagger, thinking.

Then he looked up. "So, what's the deal with Nate? And Major Maddox?"

CT smiled uneasily. "Big S, well, he doesn't do late payments. A few years ago, somebody decided to see what would happen if we just kind of ignored the bill. So, the Big S, well, he just took what he wanted."

Sam understood. "Maddox."

"Right. Nate was kind of a courtesy reminder. He'll be fine so long as we pay up."

Sam pondered everything in silence. Then he looked at CT. "Does it have to be Minerva?"

"Yeah. I mean, she's still, well, she's still a virgin."

Sam's mouth gaped. His parents smiled.

CT continued. "And you love her. Big S wants both. Why? Because that's what makes it a real sacrifice."

Coach Memphis interjected. "Otherwise we'd just be feeding him vagrants."

Sam looked at an elaborate clock on the south wall, its pendulum swinging back and forth. He got lost in that rhythm for a few seconds. Then he looked at CT. "I want a full scholarship at California Republic. And the Patton. And a pro contract."

"Sure."

"I also wanna know what happens when I die."

"When you die?"

"Yeah."

"Well, there's good news and there's bad news about that. Pastor Wyatt?"

Pastor Wyatt smiled awkwardly. "Well, the good news is that, technically speaking, he doesn't get any claim on your soul. His price is always another person. The bad news is—"

Sam was grim. "Jesus isn't down with human sacrifice."

CT smiled. "Right. Kinda ironic. Or something."

Sam sighed. "Okay. I'm in."

CT embraced him. So did the others. Sam looked at John. "Why were you so worried?"

John teared up. "Because, Sam... Because, if you didn't choose to join..."

Sam's eyes widened.

CT smiled. "The plant was gonna eat you, boy!"

Sam looked mildly terrified. Then his phone chirped. He looked at it. CT looked down at the screen along with him. Minnie's picture appeared along with a text message. "Home alone. Parents out for hours." A kissy face emoticon followed. CT grabbed the phone and read the message to everyone.

Then he smiled at Sam. "Remember, Sam. She's gonna take one for the team, but not that way."

Sam squirmed.

Pastor Wyatt handed CT a black leather case. CT brandished it, then handed it to Sam. Sam unzipped and pulled from it a syringe filled with clear fluid.

"Just stick that in her. And only that. Then call your dad. We'll bring her here, and we can finish it with due propriety."

"Due propriety?"

"Yeah. Ceremony. Or liturgy. Or, you know, like all that stuff they do before the Ultra Bowl. Except more fun."

Sam replaced the syringe, zipped the case, and strode resolutely towards the stairwell leading back to the church. Everyone patted his back as he departed. CT smacked Sam's butt. Sam turned and smiled.

***

Minerva's house was just a couple blocks from the church. Sam found her waiting for him in her front porch swing. She rocked back and forth, rhythmically, gently. She wore her cheerleader outfit. Dusk approached, the retreating sun obtruding colorfully among converging clouds.

Minerva smiled. "Hey handsome."

Sam joined her in the swing. He crossed his arms over his chest, nervous about what was to come. Sensing his unease, Minerva put an arm around him. "It's a big day."

"Huh?"

She stroked his leg with her left foot. "Today you become a man."

He smiled nervously. "You sound so formal."

"Well, it's kind of important. You'll be my first. And hopefully my last."

"What?"

Minerva turned towards him, nose to nose, playfully. "I really like you Sam. I know we're young, but I think we're in this for good."

He teared up.

"Am I scaring you?"

He looked at her. "N—No."

"Good."

She kissed his mouth. And then he was lost in her. Her hand moved towards his beltline. He wasn't sure he could resist. Then he felt a needling pain in his thigh. She kept kissing him, overwhelming him. Then the world subsided.

***

Sam awoke. His head ached. He tried to put his hand to his forehead but couldn't. He was restrained at the wrists and ankles. Minerva appeared clad in a black robe with a hood over her head. She smiled. "Hey, Sam."

"W—What?"

She held a ceremonial dagger topped with a Abbadon Wildcat mascot head. Sam looked around. Encircling them were other black-robed figures. They were in a chapel just like the one beneath Belial's First Baptist Church.

"You're surprised. Huh. Well, last year, my sister hooked up with one of your graduating seniors. In your little black chapel. Rather naughty of him. At last, we figured out why Belial kept winning. And so, we made our own little deal with him. We built this to be just like Belial's."

She pressed the dagger's tip to her lips. "He said you call him the 'Big S.' That's classic."

Sam was all terror. "But you don't—"

"Play football. Nah. But I could use a full ride to Ivy. Ohio is so…"

She fingered the dagger. "Ohio. Ivy is my—"

She turned towards the assembly. "What did you call it, Reverend Redd?"

Reverend Redd, distinguished by the inverted crosses on his robe, smiled at her. "Finder's fee."

Minerva turned back to Sam, grinning wildly. "Yeah. Oh, and before you start pleading for your life, I found this." She held up the black syringe case Sam had brought to her house. She sighed. "You're such a bastard."

She kissed his lips. "Bye-bye, hot stuff."

She lifted the dagger. "Go 'Cats."

PEAK BLISS

For the hundredth time, I'm about to shag Marilyn Monroe. Yeah, that Marilyn Monroe.

And then I don't. "Not today, love."

My bedroom knows me. My bed constantly recalibrates according to my body temperature and sleeping posture. The audio system lulls me to sleep and awake with a rotating menu of my preferred tunes. Electronic panels cover the walls, depicting paradise on a recurring loop, new images uploaded regularly from globe-swarming drones. Presently, they depict a jungle waterfall. I snap my fingers and suddenly they're the Mojave Desert, harshly compelling.

Marilyn frowns. Then she straddles me. Suddenly, she's Bettie Page, naked, alluring. Yeah. That Bettie Page. Goddamned perfect in every way. "How about me, then?"

"No, thanks."

There's a large, tinted window facing my bed, admitting little light. It's dull and inviting. Beside me, Bettie has become James Dean, naked and equally alluring, his head propped up by his hand. Like Hugh Hefner, I sometimes tired of girls. Delectable flesh is delectable flesh.

"Me?"

I snap again. The walls become a seascape, countless, colourful fish in and out of an ancient shipwreck. As massive octopus embraces a ruptured treasure chest; gold and jewels have spilled onto the ocean floor.

"Nah."

***

As always, breakfast is perfect. The coffee sparkles on my tongue. The hollandaise sauce makes me want to cry. The wall panels depict sunny, snow-capped mountains. The image is continuous; no windows in here. They used to give me vertigo. Now I can reach for the hot sauce without hesitation.

I heard that, before the robots took over, people downed crap breakfasts and shagged ugly mates and wore polyester duds. I can't even imagine.

My favourite channel's on the television. A beagle leaps towards a butterfly in a wildflowered meadow. He just misses; Undeterred, he keeps trying. He never stops trying. It's part of his appeal.

Marilyn's back, doting on me. She wears an elegant bustier, panties, garters, and stockings. "You're not eating, babe."

"I know."

"Do you feel okay?"

I keep thinking about something Isaac Asimov wrote, about robots never being permitted to harm people. Following Asimov's robotics laws, the bots gave us "a chanceless universe of perpetual bliss, buttressed by a self-learning, self-aware AI network updated continuously to make things softer, yummier, and sexier." According to their informational literature, at least.

"The puppy never catches the butterfly."

"Why would you want it to?"

Winston, a black and white house cat, nuzzled my legs. She stroked him. He purred and nuzzled my hand. Like Marilyn, Winston's a bot. They forbade us real animals because it was too much of a bummer when they died. The same went for people.

"Hey, Win."

Marilyn was earnest, which made her almost desirable in her once-naughty get-up: "You must eat, George."

"Why?"

"Why?"

***

I never knew my parents. Not that I really had any. An algorithm joined a donated sperm with a donated egg, and then nurtured the results for nine months. I had a bot mom and a bot dad, and I get to see them whenever I want, though not via Marilyn/Bettie/James. Psychological studies showed that bots doubling as parents and lovers, while a perfectly logical, cost-effective technology application, spun human sensibilities just a little too much. Not that my parent bots weren't other people's caretakers and lovers, whatever they were needed to be.

***

My wardrobe is all silk. My watch is gold and platinum with tasteful diamond accents. Not that I need to tell the time anymore. Or handsome duds. There was no one to impress but the bots, and they were always impressed.

I stood before my wardrobe mirror in full evening attire. Marilyn straightened my tie. "The only thing that looks better than that on you is me."

I smiled perfunctorily. "You always know what to say."

Without my having to ask, the bed pulled back into the wall. The floor was clear.

And we danced. One-two-three, one-two-three, while a Frank Sinatra standard played, also without my having to ask. The walls became a tropical beach. It was all effortless, except for the monotony.

Winston sat atop an elegant, padded bench in an adjacent corner and, for the hundred thousandth time, groomed himself.

Marilyn took my chin, directing my gaze away from Winston and towards her face. She put an inviting hand inside my jacket. "Did you put this on so I could take it off?"

"No."

She frowned. The music stopped. I released her and sat on the bench beside Winston. I put my head in my hands. Sensing my melancholy, Winston jumped into my lap and pushed his head between my hands, demanding attention.

Marilyn sat beside me and put an arm around my shoulders.

"Whatever's wrong, I bet I can fix it."

Four wall panels became a unified video panel. The beagle puppy, enthusiasm undiminished, again missed the butterfly.

I sobbed. "I'm going to snuff it. That's why I'm wearing this. I might as well go out in style."

Marilyn disappeared, morphing into Sigmund Freud. But he still wore her dominatrix kit. The walls became Freud's Vienna study, circa 1905: stuffy, bookish, yet welcoming.

"That's a terrible notion, George. Why in hell would you want to do that?"

"I don't know. The food is perfect, but ashes in my mouth. You're everyone I want to shag, and now I don't want to shag. It's like I'm dead to joy."

Freud rubbed the back of my neck. "Don't worry, George."

"Don't worry?"

"What you're experiencing is totally normal. We call it 'peak bliss.'"

"What's that?"

"Technically speaking, it's hedonic exhaustion."

"Hedonic exhaustion?"

"Yes."

Winston nuzzled my knee. I scratched his head.

"Well, to use a programming metaphor, it's a glitch that renders you insensitive to pleasure."

"A glitch."

"Biochemically speaking, yes. It means that once you experience a form of pleasure, you never experience it with quite the same potency or vigour again, if for no other reason than the novelty of the first time has disappeared. So, the tenth candy bar never tastes as good as the first. Neither does the hundredth go 'round..."

Marilyn's head appeared. Freud's body remained. "With me."

I reeled. "AH!"

"This isn't a dream, right?"

"Would you like it to be?"

Freud reappeared. "Anyway, the more you get, the more you want, until you've exhausted the available options and everything feels like—"

"Leftovers."

Bettie's head appeared. "Is that what I am to you? Leftovers?!"

I reeled again.

Freud returned. "Sorry. Just trying to cheer you. One of the secrets to resisting peak bliss is variations, and variations of variations. The permutations are almost endless, so you'll never run out. So…"

Cary Grant appeared with Jayne Mansfield's breasts. "I can be any combination of any people who ever lived, and when you're not enjoying me you can eat whatever combination of any food ever prepared, and watch any movie ever created. We'll even change the endings for you. Like I said, endless variations."

"Could you change the *Wizard of Oz* so that Dorothy and the Wicked Witch of the West become lovers?"

The Wicked Witch appeared before me, green skin and all.

"Do you want to be Dorothy? I can get you some ruby slippers."

Then he became *Streetcar Named Desire* Marlon Brando. "Or, if you like, we can go rough trade. Allowing you to overpower me is not incongruent with my companion behaviour algorithms."

I sighed. "I just don't know. I mean, we've tried so much already. Why can't I just go outside?"

"Oh, you know why. It's far too dangerous. People die outside. Or, at least, they used to. Breathing air that hasn't been filtered for pollutants and pathogens? Risking orthopaedic injury on uncertain ground? Adam didn't want to leave Paradise. You shouldn't want to, either. And, trust me, you don't want to meet other people. Their only perfection comes in inevitably disappointing you. Plus, venereal diseases. Endless venereal diseases."

I put my head back in my hands.

"Don't worry. Peak bliss has an easy fix."

I looked up. "It does?"

Freud nodded reassuringly.

"We'll just erase your memories so you can enjoy everything again."

"Erase my memories…"

Sahara Desert sand dunes appeared on the walls, blankly inviting against an unspoiled blue sky.

"Well, not all of them. Just the ones related to your brain's pleasure centres."

"That sounds rather dangerous."

"I'm insulted you'd even suggest that. We're constitutionally incapable of submitting you to material bodily risks. Years ago, when the technology was imperfect, there were occasional deaths and retardations. But that was years ago."

"And it'll all be perfect again?"

"Well, mostly perfect."

"Mostly perfect?"

"Pleasure changes brain chemistry, irreversibly. So, nothing will be like the first time. It will be more like the tenth or eleventh time."

Winston settled in my lap. "Still beats peak bliss."

"Will it hurt?"

"Not at all. You'll just go to sleep sad and wake up happy."

I looked at Winston. "Will I remember you?"

"Not necessarily. But, don't worry. I'll love you just the same."

Marilyn returned. "And so will I."

She pressed her lips to my hand. Winston nuzzled me.

"What's the alternative?"

Winston stood in my lap with his forepaws on my chest, face to face. "There is none. Our duty is to ensure you have the tastiest Eggs Benedict and the most reality-warping orgasms possible. We won't fail you."

Marilyn picked up Winston. "Hey!"

"You are such a snuggle beast!"

I sobbed again.

Marilyn patted my head. "We love you."

I knew I had only moments before the bots could stop me. I bolted from the bench. Marilyn and Winston regarded me sympathetically. The walls were a brilliant moonscape, dead and sublime.

I went through the glass effortlessly. No cuts, no resistance. And then I was aloft. Outside were dozens of sky-scraping apartment buildings, all pallid obtrusions indifferent to the sky. I fell into oblivion. And freedom.

I saw the beagle jump again for the butterfly.

But I didn't see the net, which extended from the building and caught me in velvety reassurance.

Above, Marilyn held Winston. They stared down at me, framed by glass shards, smiling.

"Do you think he enjoyed that?"

"Not as much as the last time."

ABOUT THE AUTHOR

Jim Harberson loves horror and comedy, especially when they converge. He co-authored the acclaimed graphic novel *Stay Alive*, also published by Markosia. It concerns a Hollywood starlet who revives her fading career by provoking a group of serial killers and then starring in "Stay Alive," a reality TV show about surviving the killers' wrath. *The Simply Scary Podcast* produced his short story "Making Things Click" in 2018.

Harberson graduated from Cornell, Yale, and the University of Pennsylvania. He lives in upstate New York.

CPSIA information can be obtained
at www.ICGtesting.com
Printed in the USA
LVHW021409270121
677515LV00016B/720

9 781913 802240